Ice King

ICE

KING

By Ernestine N. Byrd

Illustrated by Marilyn Miller

Charles Scribner's Sons

New York

$\dfrac{B}{C\text{-}1}$

For permission to quote Eskimo words, grateful
acknowledgement is made to
Doubleday and Company, Inc.
From *Kaah-da* by Donald B. MacMillan.
Copyright 1930 by Doubleday and Company, Inc.
Reprinted by permission of the publisher.

Printed in the United States of America
Library of Congress Catalog Card Number 65-18941

To my daughter and son,
Barbara Lee Anderson and
Cdr. Newton Phillips Byrd, Jr. (Ret.)

CONTENTS

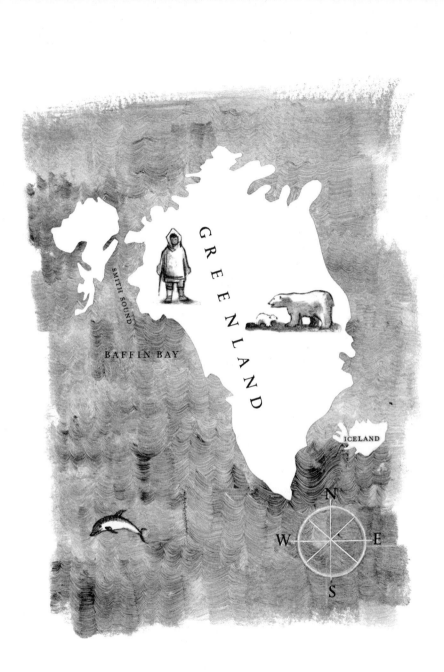

GREENLAND

SMITH SOUND

BAFFIN BAY

ICELAND

N
W E
S

CHAPTER 1

A White World

Atu stood looking around him. It was the first time he had been out of his snow den and the strange world, at first puzzling, filled him with curiosity and excitement. Here was a den without walls, one large enough to let him run and jump as much as he pleased. Everything was so new and exciting he forgot he was hungry until his mother sat down and leaned against a bank of ice. Nothing was more important than warm milk in his belly, and in two quick leaps he was huddled in the shelter of her huge forepaws while his eyes explored the tumbled whiteness of new horizons.

Teecha was even more interested in the outside world. She had mated the previous June, and the big male bear of her affections had stayed with her until August. Then they had gone their separate ways. After that, she had wandered alone, eating all the seals she could kill so that her ribs, bones, muscular frame and belly would be soaked with fat before she hibernated. In November, when she sensed her approaching motherhood, she went far out on the vast ice fields of Baffin Bay below Smith Sound. When she found a place to her liking among tumbled piles of ice, she dug down as far as she could into the deeply drifted snow, then curled up and went to sleep. By natural instinct she knew how to place her body in this shelter so that when the freezing winds piled the snow about her, tamping it as hard as ice, a small air hole would be formed in the snow dome over the den. Snug and warm she drowsed the days away, waiting for the birth of her Nannuk.

In the dark January world of sub-zero cold, Atu was born. Though ice bears often give birth to twins, this season Teecha had only one tiny cub to care for. What a funny-looking little bear he was —not quite a foot long, almost hairless, blind, and without teeth. The first few weeks of his life he slept on his mother's big, soft, warm abdomen.

When he was five weeks old he began crawling rather clumsily over her, and when he was six weeks old his eyes opened. At seven weeks, his hair coat was not only thick and woolly, but he had enough sharp teeth to chew on his mother's ears, and this became his favorite game. When she grew tired of his chewing she would roll him over with her forepaws and wash him with her rough black tongue. He did not like to be washed, but his mother held him so lightly, yet so firmly, his fat legs could not kick themselves free.

Later in March, with the sun once more above the horizon, the ice walls of the den began to thin, allowing the pale sunlight to seep dimly through. Teecha pushed against the walls until one side gave way, leaving a big, jagged hole. After stepping through, she turned and lifted Atu out by the loose skin on the back of his neck, then she dropped him gently on the ice. This was his introduction into the world.

Atu liked what he saw, and so did his mother, for she refused to let him nurse any longer. She pushed him aside and got up. Months of hibernation without food and her cub's constant nursing had reduced her huge body; her yellowish-white coat hung in thin, loose folds over gaunt ribs. She needed a seal to fill her empty belly. Long ago she had learned about the ringed seals' igloos. A tunnel ran from the mother seal's breathing hole in the ice to a burrow of hard snow she had dug out with her heavy claws. In this burrow, or igloo, one or two woolly white pups were born—good eating for a hungry bear.

Teecha walked for several hours, sniffing long and carefully around small hummocks resembling seal igloos, but her keen sense of smell told her she would have to go farther out on the ice. She did not want to do this, hungry as she was, for past experience had taught her that the lighter days brought the hunting season, and with it human enemies. Mounting an ice bump, she turned her long, slender head from side to side, testing the air currents at a higher level with deep, pulling breaths.

Atu sensed that his mother was searching for something, but he had no idea what it was. His interest quickened when she moved forward slowly, her yellowish-white body swaying slightly in a rolling motion. As she passed him, he nipped her heels. She turned quickly and bunted him. Though she hardly touched him, he lost his balance and rolled over. Jumping to his feet, he nipped her again. If she meant to play, he was ready.

But it seemed that his mother did not want to play. Instead, she nudged him to one side, a gentle reminder that he was to leave her alone. Then she went on, this time walking faster. Atu followed. Her big feet and his small feet made crunching noises on the snow. Teecha's long, rolling strides carried her at such a fast pace Atu could hardly keep up with her. He soon grew tired and refused to go another step.

Teecha continued on. It was not long, though, before she looked back. Atu was sitting down, his nose pointed to the sky, about to let out a mournful bawl. She stared at him for a few moments, then returned and let him climb on her back.

Soon a strong wind came up, blowing snow crystals in their faces. Teecha found shelter under a big snow mound and Atu slid from her back. She scooped out a hole in the deep drifts and curled her body around him. In a few minutes both were asleep.

The next day they resumed their journey. With the returning sunlight Teecha followed the ice pack north toward bays and inlets where she had hunted in the past. Atu noticed that his mother constantly sniffed the air. Her nose twitched as long as she was awake. His own food was her rich milk, so it was not until she caught her first seal that he learned what his mother ate.

Trotting by her side, his small feet took two

steps to one of her big ones. The breeze was blowing toward them and Atu's sensitive nostrils picked up the oily pungence of Netsik, the little ringed seals of the Arctic. It was a strange but interesting odor.

His mother seemed to be testing the odor, too. Then she looked at him and growled. He had never heard her growl quite like this before and sensed it was a warning of some kind. He stood quietly waiting to see what it meant. When she suddenly lay down, he stretched out beside her, quick to obey. She reached over and bunted him, growling again. Now he understood. It meant that he was to pay strict attention to what she was about to do. He shivered with excitement, expecting some new kind of game.

Gradually, by bunting and nudging and sniffing, he learned that the strange odor filling his nostrils came only when the wind blew toward them. What the odor was, he did not know, but he sensed it was important to his mother for she covered her black nose with her forepaws, turning under the black-tipped claws so that only the yellowish-whiteness of her body could be seen. He lay beside her, covering his own nose and claws in the same manner, his bright eyes peeking above them. His mother's warning glances kept him from wrig-

16

gling nervously. How cautious she was, inching her way slowly forward with her hind legs. The mystery of this game deepened with every movement of her body.

Teecha approached the seal's Atluk, or breathing hole, with great care, for the seal was lying beside it, no doubt enjoying the returning sunlight. Atu's excitement mounted. What was his mother going to do? He was almost to the point of jumping up when she suddenly gave a tremendous lunge and grabbed the seal. With one quick blow from her paw she killed it. Then she began tearing at the blubber.

Now Atu bounded to her side. He sniffed the smooth, dark head and the bristly whiskers of the seal. Up close, its odor was appetizing and he wanted to taste it. His mother gave him a small chunk of the warm, oily blubber, and after sniffing it curiously he gobbled it down. It tasted so good that he wanted a second helping, so she gave him another small piece, but she refused to give him more. She knew that too much blubber at first would make him sick. Atu licked his paws and smacked. Now he understood the "game" they had been playing. His mother had been teaching him how to catch a seal.

Each hour seemed to bring a change in the weather. Heavy cloud formations cast a grayish light over the white world, but when the pale sun broke through, the air felt warmer. Then Teecha liked to curl up among big chunks of ice and sleep. Sometimes Atu snuggled beside her, but more often he played games of his own invention, rolling like a dog and kicking up loose snow.

One day Teecha found a crack in the ice several feet wide. She jumped into the "lead" and swam around, now and then rolling her body and slapping the water playfully. Atu watched her with growing interest, but he had no intention of joining her. When she jumped up beside him and shook her oily white fur from head to tail he began backing away. Becoming suspicious he ran, but he was not fast enough. His mother caught him and bumped his shoulder hard. This meant that he was to return with her at once. And to make sure that he got started in the right direction, she delivered a nudge on his small rump which shoved him forward.

Atu walked back slowly, grumbling. When they reached the water his mother waited for him to get in, but he dug his claws into the ice. Teecha gave him a gentle push to encourage him. When this was not effective, a more forceful one followed, this time hard enough to make him lose his balance and fall in, head first. He came to the top, kicking

18

and splashing and sputtering for breath, his mouth open, bawling angrily.

Teecha slipped into the water beside him and bunted him playfully. Atu climbed on her back as fast as he could. Now he was safe. His mother swam around until he was less fearful, then with a quick sideways motion, she rolled him from her back. It was so unexpected that he landed in the water, sputtering and bobbing. His legs turned around like small windmills, stirring the water into a white foam. After making a few chopping motions forward, he headed for the ice. His mother followed, and when he crawled out she pushed him in again. She continued to do this until he stayed in the water and swam around for several minutes, then she let him get out.

Atu shook himself and looked at her for approval. She seemed satisfied and licked his face. He sprang at her, hoping she was in a mood to play and forget about swimming, but she lay down and closed her eyes. He flopped beside her and began nudging and biting her ears. His teeth were so sharp she rolled over and cuffed him. After that he was more careful, but he had made her notice him and that was what he wanted.

As they lazed in the sun, nipping each other and wrestling playfully, Teecha's eyes suddenly flashed with fear and her body stiffened. She had caught the scent of Eskimo dogs. She was not afraid of the dogs, but her deadly enemy, man, would not be far behind.

Jumping to her feet, she picked up Atu by the back of his neck just as a pack of vicious dogs swarmed over a snow mound, surrounding them. With long white fangs snapping, the dogs were frightful-looking creatures. Atu tried to pull his short legs even closer to his round little belly as his mother's deadly claws lashed out at the dogs. Slapping one, she lifted it high in the air. It fell on the snow and rolled over, howling. With a swift movement of her body, still holding Atu, she leaped over a more cautious animal moving away from her and streaked up the side of a hummock, her hairy padded feet clinging easily to the shining ice. As her hindquarters disappeared over the top, rifle shots rang out and bullets spit up chunks of ice, adding to the already terrifying noise and confusion.

Teecha ran until she sensed it was safe to stop, then she put Atu down on the snow. She had held him in her jaws all the way. Rising on her hind feet, she tested the air currents in all directions. When she did not pick up the scent of her human enemies, she dropped to all fours and bunted Atu lovingly. Hunger had almost cost her the life of her cub as well as her own, but he was safe now. That was all she wanted. She would kill for him, and even sacrifice her own life that he might live.

Slurping his face gently, Teecha scooped out a bed in the snow and they cuddled up together. Atu felt safe with her warm body against his own, but he would never forget the big, vicious dogs, or the noise and confusion that had filled him with terror. He did not understand it, but he sensed its deadliness.

CHAPTER 2

The Strange Bear

Day after day, Teecha and Atu hunted seals and played together. Atu saw Ookpik, the white Arctic owl, perched on a spire of ice like a sentinel, just out of reach of his inquisitive paws. Ookuda, the Arctic hare, white as the snow, raced swiftly in front of them, disappearing into the low-lying hills in the distance. Atu sensed it was foolish to chase Ookuda. It could run too fast.

Though Atu and his mother had traveled many miles, they had never seen any other bears. Now

23

they met a mother bear and her two cubs. Atu was excited. Looking quickly at his mother, he wondered what she meant to do about these strangers. She did not appear to be interested in getting acquainted but she watched the other big bear closely.

Atu wanted to play and trotted over to the cubs before his mother could stop him. They returned his offer of friendship by suddenly pouncing on him, their sharp teeth and claws pinching and raking his hide before he could get away. Upset and angry, he ran back to his mother to be comforted. Teecha licked his face and nudged him into good humor again, then pushed him aside and walked away. Atu trotted after her, bawling at the top of his voice for more attention, but she ignored him.

After that, he darted between her front legs and tried to nurse as they walked along. Nursing in this way was not easy and he was forced to give up, but he continued to walk between her front legs. He listened as she made rumbling, singing noises deep in her throat. They were sounds that he liked, so he made them, too.

The bears moved along almost silently, except for the soft crunching of their hairy padded feet against the snow. Then Teecha suddenly stopped. She appeared nervous, uncertain. She pushed Atu behind her, growling. She tested the air currents, moving her head from side to side. Atu trembled. Was she scenting their animal enemies? He watched until her restless movements quieted. When she seemed satisfied that danger was not present, she growled again, but this time playfully.

Then Teecha whirled and ran up a hillside. The snow was covered with an icy crust, and it was slippery. When she reached the top she sat down, gave herself a push, and coasted all the way to the bottom, landing in a cloud of flying crystals right in front of Atu. Blowing snow from her face, she bounded up the hill again.

This time, Atu followed. They sat down, side by side, gave a push and away they went. Atu rolled most of the way to the bottom, landing upside down in an undignified heap. Wiping the snow from his eyes, he stared at his mother. She was looking back at him. He shook himself, got to his feet and ran over and nipped her, ready for another slide.

They climbed the hill over and over until their romp was brought to an abrupt end by the sound of guns in the distance. Terrified, Teecha pushed Atu ahead of her, urging him to hurry. When he did not run fast enough she placed her head against his rump and shoved him forward. His legs were still not strong enough to carry him speedily over the snow so she let him climb on her back. Then she almost flew over the ice toward a protective jumble of hummocks. Once inside, she stopped and checked the wind currents. Growling low, she stood quietly, as if listening. When she seemed satisfied there was no danger, she let Atu get down. She licked his face and he stopped trembling. The touch of her rough black tongue reassured him.

Teecha hunted for seals constantly. She must have game and plenty of it. One day she led Atu to a grounded iceberg, one that was frozen into a mass of sea ice. There were always cracks around the bergs made by the rise and fall of the tide. Little shrimp-like creatures lived there and the seals fed on them. The seals also used the cracks for breathing holes. As Teecha approached downwind, Atu followed. He was excited, for this hunt was different. There was no seal in view, only a mound of ice that towered into the sky. How could his mother catch game she could not see? She might smell it, but he could not.

Drifts of snow were piled against the sides of the berg. Atu watched as Teecha hid behind one. As usual her long, slender head weaved slowly back and forth, her sensitive nostrils checking the air. Then she crawled around the side of the drift until she was near an ice crack, and lay quietly.

26

Suddenly she slipped into the depths of the icy water. Down quickly. Up quickly—with a seal in her mouth! Tossing it onto the ice she climbed up and glanced at Atu. This was his invitation to join her. Atu ran forward. But in his excitement his claws caught in an ice crack and over he flipped, skimming round and round like a top, then rolling into the water. Down he went into the black depths around the berg.

Teecha plunged in after him. Grabbing him by the back of the neck she pulled him to the surface and tossed him onto the ice. Then she climbed out and licked him briskly all over. Atu weaved back and forth dizzily, his eyes blinking wetly at his mother, his mouth open, bawling with terror.

Angry with his clumsiness, she cuffed his ears. She knew that the rise and fall of a strong tide underneath the ice could suck the body of a grown bear against an iceberg and crush it. Only long experience, and the perfect timing of her own instincts, had taught her how to hunt seals around bergs. To impress this lesson on him she cuffed his ears again and growled. Atu understood.

Teecha turned to the seal and began tearing at the blubber. At first Atu did not feel like eating, but his mother kept smacking so loudly that his belly stopped its nervous jerking and he gobbled

27

down a large chunk of fat. When their meal was over, Atu and his mother lay down side by side, Teecha on her back, forepaws dangling limply above her broad chest, Atu on his side. He kept licking his paws and smacking, for grease was still on them and it tasted good.

The sky was clear and the sun, Sukanuk, warm. Teecha scratched her sides and belly with her long black claws, pulling absent-mindedly at ragged patches of fur. Atu felt sleepy. He rolled over and snuggled one forepaw under the heavy folds of her neck. He loved to sleep this way. Making a sucking noise with his tongue, he was soon deep in slumber. Teecha went to sleep, too, but not before she placed one forepaw protectively across his small body.

Several hours later when they awoke, Sukanuk was low on the horizon, coloring the darkening sky with streaks of reddish-gold. The ice shimmered in the glow of the setting sun, sending off sparks of color like brilliant yellow diamonds.

When they came to another ice crack, Teecha jumped in the water, but Atu hesitated. However, when his mother glanced at him, he jumped in hurriedly. Landing with a loud splash, he climbed aboard her back and she carried him around. They played until they caught the scent of another bear, then his mother flipped him from her back and left the water at once.

Atu saw the reason for her sudden departure, a big ice bear, much larger than his mother. Curious, he got out of the water. Swiftly his mother moved in between him and the newcomer, a deep growl rolling up from the depths of her throat. Atu knew that growl. It was a warning. But why?

Teecha knew the answer. Sometimes, at first, males resent their small offspring and try to hurt them. But Boc did not seem jealous or resentful. He looked at Atu as if he were quite interested in this small replica of himself, then he ambled over to Teecha and nosed her in an affectionate manner. He paid no further attention to Atu.

Atu did not like this stranger fondling his mother, but he sensed a closeness between them that he did not yet understand. He liked their actions even less when they bumped each other and wrestled. They paid no attention to him until much later when his mother returned and nosed him. Then, with a firm bunt, she pushed him toward the big, strange bear. This was her way of introducing him to his father.

Though Atu's natural instinct was to get acquainted, he felt that he would be just as happy if this new parent went away. He was quite satisfied

with his mother. But Teecha pushed him forward
again with a bunt hard enough to land him at his
father's feet in an undignified sprawl. Angered, Atu
jumped up and blew through his nose, then stared
sullenly at the big male.

Boc stared back, as if wondering what to do
next. Atu was the first to decide. He started backing up. His father followed slowly, shaking his head
and stomping one forefoot playfully.

Atu continued backing up until he stood be-
neath his mother's front legs. From this safe retreat
he peeked out, his eyes filled with a mixture of
curiosity and resentment—curiosity, because his
father was so huge; resentment, because he acted
as if he were boss.

Uncertain what to do next, Atu stood quietly while his mother licked the top of his head. He understood that she was trying to soothe his ruffled feelings, and under her loving touch his anger and jealousy began to melt. Perhaps he should nose his father who looked friendly.

While he tried to decide, his mother walked away, leaving him unprotected. Atu opened his mouth to bawl, but thought better of it when he saw his parents jump into the water. He watched as they playfully boxed and wrestled. He could have

joined them, but he stood sulking. Now he liked his father even less. He had taken his mother away again.

Atu wandered off by himself. He kept expecting his mother to come after him. Since he could catch her body odor in the air, he knew she could scent him, too. He stared at the white world around him. It looked lonely without his mother. Perhaps he should join them.

As he topped a snow mound he saw them walking slowly across the ice, sniffing the air expectantly. It seemed they had caught the odor of seal and were going hunting. He was hungry. He wanted to nurse. Now he would have to wait until his mother made a kill.

Later, Teecha returned, a chunk of seal fat in her mouth. She dropped it in front of Atu and he gobbled it down. But he wanted milk even more. He butted Teecha until she sat down and let him nurse. Holding her close with his forepaws, he kicked one hind leg, completely happy. His mother belonged to him again.

When Boc returned he smelled of seal fat, too. He leaned down and sniffed Atu. All at once their relationship seemed warm and natural, and Atu was no longer angry or jealous. Reaching up, he licked Boc.

32

CHAPTER 3

Blood on the Snow

Atu and his mother and father played together until
the bright, sunlit day settled into a gray twilight,
then they went on their way again, Boc in the lead.
It was not long before Atu grew tired and began to
bawl. He wanted to go to sleep. His mother paid
little attention to him, his father none at all. But
Atu was used to having his own way, so he kept on
bawling until his mother stopped and scooped out a
bed for them. Lying down, she curled her body
around him, and soon both were asleep.

Boc continued on. He disappeared into the
snowy world as quietly as he had first appeared,

33

and they did not see him for several days. When they met him again he acted as if he had never seen them before, and was not interested in getting acquainted.

Such an attitude was confusing to Atu. But as the days passed he learned that his father came and went as he pleased. He had his own way of living and it did not depend on his family. Sometimes Boc was in an amiable mood. When he was, he played with Atu and Teecha, but more often he remained aloof, even though he hunted only a short distance away.

Atu gradually sensed that adult males were independent of their mates and offspring. When they wanted to be with the family group they made an appearance. When they wanted to be alone, they went away.

Watching his father walking toward them now, Atu felt a shiver of excitement. He and his mother went to meet the big white bear striding so confidently, so majestically across the ice. This time Boc seemed unusually affectionate, nuzzling and bunting him. Atu enjoyed this extra attention. It made him feel important. He fondled his father in return, a warm thrill running from his cold little nose to the tip of his short tail.

As usual Boc wanted to be on the move. He led

the way, Teecha by his side, their yellowish-white pelts stirring and rippling as they walked. Atu followed. Feeling very gay, he chased imaginary playmates and dug in the snow, making the crystals fly. Quite unexpectedly he flushed an Arctic hare. It bounded off, and he pursued. But Ookuda was too fast. Atu soon lost sight of his quarry, discovering at the same time that he had wandered far from his parents. He trotted briskly for a short distance, sniffing the air exploringly. A strange, yet vaguely familiar odor filled his nostrils. Eyes dilating with fear, he stood on his hind legs for a stronger scent, and froze.

Coming toward him, on the run, were Eskimo dogs! Atu was terrified. With one quick glance behind him he whirled and ran. If he could reach his parents in time . . .

Boc and Teecha had caught the odor of the dogs long before they heard them. They could have escaped easily, but Atu was not with them and they would not leave him behind.

Just as Teecha and Boc set off after him, Atu sailed over a snow mound, bawling with terror. He was running as fast as his short legs would carry him, the dogs on his flying heels, snapping their long teeth, trying at every jump to grab one of his hind legs. But he managed to keep several leaps ahead of

35

his four-legged enemies and reached his mother in time to slide under her belly.

Boc charged, his immense forearms slapping at the dogs with killing force. Teecha was busy protecting Atu, slapping at the dogs in turn, trying her best to kill them. In the midst of this barking, yelping, snarling melee of dogs and bears, three Eskimos topped a low hummock.

By now the scene below was a mass of confusion, noisy and deadly confusion. Two overly brave dogs were dead. Two others were limping around and howling. All were growling, beside themselves with hate and pain, but they still showed

no fear. Now they were more cautious. They seemed to know that they had these bears trapped and they intended to stay until they were either called off by their owners, or rifle shots put an end to their big white enemies.

Taking aim, the lead Eskimo shot Boc. The bullet caught him in the shoulder and knocked him sprawling. With a howl of rage and pain he struggled to his feet, throwing his enormous body in front of Atu and Teecha. His roar-like growls warned them to run.

Teecha whirled, but she could not escape either. Two Eskimos faced her, guns pointed in her direction. Terrified for Atu and enraged, she charged. A bullet felled her.

The crack of another rifle sounded. Down went Boc again, rolling over and over. Struggling to his feet, he bit savagely at his shoulder. Burning with rage and pain, he charged his human enemies, heading up the hummock toward them. Though mortally wounded, he continued upward, digging his great black claws into the ice, his small, dark eyes now red with hate, centered on his destroyers. With one last, convulsive movement he tried to reach them, but life was flowing out too rapidly. He collapsed, blood spurting from his mouth and chest, forming a spreading pool of red on the snow.

Off to one side lay Teecha, strangely crumpled and still.

The blasts from the rifle had frightened Atu so badly that he could not move, but when his mother did not get up he ran to her side and flung himself on her body. Hugging her close, he cried the deep, hoarse sobs that young bears sometimes utter. He wanted her to stand up and fight. But his mother did not open her eyes. Her big head did not move in answer to his wails and the frantic pushing of his forepaws. Not understanding why she did not respond, he continued to push and wail and sob out his grief.

Growling with hate, one of the Eskimo dogs got loose and attacked Atu. Death would have followed had not one of the men quickly intervened. He reached his sled dog in time to wield a rawhide whip. The dog yelped, but it let go.

Atu got to his feet, dazed and shaken, blood running from his shoulder where the long fangs had ripped into his tender flesh. He stuck out his upper lip and blew through his nose, his way of warning that he was not afraid to fight.

Komi, the Eskimo boy, heard his father say, "We'd better lasso the cub now."

Before Atu was aware of what was happening, a skin line was thrown over him. Filled with rage,

he fought wildly. As his body strained and twisted under the rawhide thongs, he was tied securely on top of a sledge. He kept straining at the thongs, bawling out his growls, so angry and filled with hate that he did not feel the pain in his shoulder. He wanted to rip and tear and kill.

Tears filled Komi's eyes. Ashamed, he wiped them away quickly. Eskimos did not cry over dead ice bears. But at the moment he felt sorry for Ahtuckta, who no longer had a mother. The cub's apparent grief bothered him. It was true that he had wanted a cub to play with, but not at the expense of the mother's life. When cubs were quite young they could be tamed, and this one was exactly the right age. When it got over its grief, perhaps it would forget what had happened.

"At last a young bear for you to play with, and more pants and meat for us," said his uncle as all of them looked at the dead bears. The big male filled them with awe and admiration.

"Nannuksuak. A big bear and a brave one," Komi's father answered.

Komi looked at the two bears lying in a crumpled heap on the ice. Mother bears were the bravest and most dangerous of all when they had cubs. But it seemed that this father bear had been willing to die for his young, too. They had fought and died together for one small offspring. Brave ones—he liked that. He thought he would ask his father for the spleen of each one to feed his young dogs. The bears' spleen would make the dogs even more courageous.

The Eskimos skinned the bears with their long, sharp knives and cut up the meat. Komi's dogs sat down beside him and rubbed their shaggy heads against his bear pants. They knew they would soon be rewarded for their brave stand, but they did not know how choice the reward was to be.

40

Later Komi divided the spleen, giving each dog a small portion.

"You are brave now," he told them solemnly, "but after eating this you will be even braver. Perhaps the bravest dogs in the Far North!"

Komi's father and uncle nodded gravely. They believed this legend.

During the long, rough journey home, Atu's anger gradually changed into sullenness. He tried to keep his face hidden, not wanting to look at the dogs. And most of all he did not want to look at his captors riding in the light hunting sledges ahead. They had taken his parents from him and he sensed he would never see them again.

The hunting sledges skimmed over the ice even though they were packed solidly. Komi, his father and uncle had been hunting walrus far to the south during the months of March and April. They were on their way home when the dogs had scented the bears, and now they had an abundance of fur as well as meat for the coming winter.

The dogs, hitched fan fashion to the sledges, speeded up as the long, thirty-foot whips cracked above their heads. Descendants of the northern gray or white wolves, the dogs were of different colors, some reddish-brown, others tan, black, white and gray. The gray ones, with dashes of black and pure white, were the most beautiful and the most typical of the Eskimo breeds. Strong, spirited animals, with sharp muzzles, wide-set eyes, shaggy coats and pointed ears, their bushy tails curled tightly against their backs.

The Smith Sound Eskimos were dressed in warm skins. Each wore a heavy-hooded winter coat made from blue and white fox, knee-length trousers of ice bear skin, and boots of sealskin, with stockings of Arctic hare, fur side to the foot. Mittens of sealskin with the hair left on protected their hands. The three Eskimos were warm and comfortable and supremely happy.

Komi lay breast down on his sledge, thinking about the little cub they had captured. What fun he would have with it! He had always wanted one, and now he was taking one home. First, he would tame the bear. Then they would play games together.

"He will be my friend," Komi said to himself. "He will learn to trust me."

As the dogs hurried along the smooth ice foot the Eskimos were watchful, for the turns were sharp and piles of rocks and boulders often covered the trail. Even the dogs seemed excited, thrilling to the crack of the long whips over their heads and the sound of voices calling, "Ahchook! Right! Howah! Left! Huk! Ahead!"

42

When the Eskimos finally reached their home, a rock igloo partly covered with snow, Atu was transferred to a low, circular stone pen. The thongs were removed and he was free. His body felt stiff and his mind confused. A piece of walrus meat was dropped in front of him, but he would not touch it. He continued to defy his enemies by blowing through his nose and striking at them with his fore-paws.

Komi and his father were amused.

"The cub has spirit!" the father declared.

Komi leaned over the pen and looked down at the little bear. Atu stared back with such an expression of hate in his eyes that for one moment Komi was doubtful about taming him. Then he shrugged. Of course he could tame this cub. It was still too much of a baby to stay angry long. But first, he must teach it not to be afraid of him.

Komi's father and uncle unloaded the sledges and took the meat and hides inside the igloo. Then they covered the pen with heavy driftwood boards. Tired after the long journey, they crawled through the Toksuk, or entrance to the igloo, and Komi followed.

Atu listened for what seemed like a long time, but he heard nothing except the fierce growls of the feeding dogs. How dark and lonely it was inside

43

the pen. If only he had his mother to snuggle up to. He licked the torn place on his shoulder for several minutes. His entire body felt stiff and pained him so much that he whimpered. Hanging his head, he leaned against the stone pen and hiccoughed deep, hoarse sobs, sobs that gradually became muffled, then ceased as he fell into a restless sleep of exhaustion.

CHAPTER 4

The Call of the Sea

Atu whined and pushed his forepaws against the cold stones, even in sleep still trying to snuggle up to his mother. Waking with a start, he jumped up and sniffed the icy air. How quiet it was. Not even the dogs were growling. By now his belly felt empty, and he looked at the walrus meat, eyeing it with growing interest. Sniffing it carefully, he stretched out, holding the chunk between his forepaws. The frozen meat took a lot of chewing, but he ate it all eagerly.

45

With hunger partially satisfied, all his energies were now bent toward escape. He set to work patiently searching for a chink deep enough in which to sink his claws. The stones were rough, and he tested each one as high up as he could reach until he found several he could sink his claws into. Pulling himself to the top, he pushed and pushed against the heavy driftwood planks, but he could not dislodge them. His low, impatient growls increased to bawl-like whines, but he would not give up.

Scenting the dogs, he blew through his nose. Their odor was a stench in his nostrils. It was hard to understand all that had happened, or might happen.

Where were his human enemies? Would their long sticks suddenly reach down and boom in his ears? A deep sense of loneliness swept over him. It was as if once more he saw his mother and father standing on their hind feet, challenging their enemies, bawling with rage. Now he was certain he would never see them again.

Unable to make his escape he finally curled up as near the stone wall as he could get, making low, mournful sounds. Resting his muzzle on his forepaws, he closed his eyes, his heart thumping wildly. Exhausted with fear and shaking with nervousness, he eventually dropped off into restless sleep, and he

46

did not wake up until he heard the clatter of drift-wood boards being pushed aside.

"Ahtuckta," came a soft voice.

Atu looked up. The Eskimo boy was watching him. There was a kindness in the dark eyes that reached out and melted some of the fear and distrust in Atu's heart. But the face was still the face of an enemy. He blew through his nose and slapped at it.

After a while, the face disappeared.

But the next day it reappeared, this time followed by a hand holding something.

"Ahtuckta, Ahtuckta," purred the voice, "here is something to eat." A piece of walrus meat fell beside the cub.

Again Atu blew through his nose and slapped at the hand, but sharp edge of his hate was gone. The warmth in the boy's voice made him think of his mother's low, comforting growl. And he longed to be comforted.

The third day was the same, but by the end of the week, when Komi pushed the heavy planks aside, he saw that he was making progress. The cub seemed to be waiting for him.

Atu thought the voice sounded even kinder than before, and he wondered if he could trust the hands that had the odor of man about them. Instinct warned him not to, but loneliness made him

47

reach up and carefully take the frozen meat from the Eskimo boy.

"I thought you'd come around," Komi said aloud. "You're such a baby you could not stay angry very long. Already you want to be my friend." He studied the little bear intently while he waited for him to finish eating. Then, sitting on the flat rim of the stone pen, Komi stepped down inside and lifted Atu up by the loose skin on the back of his neck. At any moment Atu could have clawed him, but his forepaws only clung to Komi's shoulders as the Eskimo boy climbed outside again. When Atu was on the ground he sensed he was free. The boy could not catch him. But when he heard the word, "Ahtuckta," in that soft, caressing voice, he stood still, quivering, undecided. He looked up, and something in the eyes of the Eskimo boy reached out and held him. Atu felt strangely comforted; thoughts of confusion, fear and hate suddenly disappeared and his body tingled and glowed. He would not run away. He would stay here.

Komi rubbed the top of Atu's head with his hand. "You could run away," he said, "and I could not stop you. But, somehow I do not think you will. You are going to be my playmate. We shall always be friends." Stubby fingers were thrust into Atu's neck, scratching the hide under his thick fur.

48

Atu liked the scratching. He had the same sensation when he rubbed his body against the ice.

"Tokoo! Look!" Komi pointed to the ice foot. "We will go down there," he said to Atu, and ran down the hillside.

Atu did not know what the words meant, but he was willing to follow his new friend. They raced along the ice foot until Komi was panting.

"Eye! Stop!" he called, and Atu, who had been outrunning his playmate, stopped, recognizing the sound of command in the boy's voice. It had the tone of his mother's growl when she wanted him to obey.

Trotting back to Komi, Atu looked into his face. What do you want? his eyes seemed to ask.

As if in answer, Komi said, "I want to look at your shoulder." Then he knelt by Atu and examined the deep, ragged tear, now red and badly swollen.

"A mean cut," Komi said. "I do not believe this part of your shoulder will ever be smooth again." He knew he could not harness the cub for several days. First, the shoulder must heal.

Jumping up, he ran along the ice foot. "Kaigit! Come here!" he called, clapping his hands, and Atu ran to him.

The two played together until Komi saw his

father and uncle coming across the ice, then he hurried to get Atu back into the pen. He wanted the cub out of reach before the dogs got home. One might get loose and hurt Ahtuckta.

But Atu refused. Freedom was too sweet. Komi got behind him and pushed. Atu dug his claws into the ice, stubbornly refusing to move, but when he glanced at Komi, who was pushing on his small rump and calling out, "Huk! Huk! Ahead! Ahead!" he saw the dogs and men coming up the hillside to the igloo. Without further argument he headed for the pen, leaped inside and cowered against the stone wall, for the dogs and men still filled him with terror.

"How did the cub get out of the pen?" Komi's father demanded.

"I took him out," Komi answered.

His father was angry. "That was a foolish and dangerous thing to do! He might have clawed you."

"He would not hurt me, ever!" Komi declared emphatically. "We are friends. We shall always be friends."

His father scowled. "Timah. It is done. Now Ahtuckta must be taken out again. The pen is to be filled with game. I'll lasso him."

"Please, Father, do not lasso him. It might frighten him. I'll get him out."

51

"Be careful," warned his father. "No one knows what a frightened young bear will do."

Komi leaned over the pen. "Tooavit! Tooavit! Hurry up! Hurry up!" he said, snapping his fingers. "You must come out again."

Atu understood what he was supposed to do, but he was not sure he wanted to get out. With the dogs and men back this was a safe place in which to stay. But his friend would not let him alone. It seemed he was to come out of the pen whether he liked it or not.

Komi's father was tired, and now he was angry.

"Get the cub out," he called, "or I'll lasso it!"

"Please, Father," Komi answered, "I'll get him out in a few minutes. Right now he is afraid. If you lasso him he might run away. Besides, where shall we keep him?"

"The cub will not run away," his father said. "Not as long as we feed him. Now get him out!"

Komi tried to hurry, but his coaxing had no effect on Atu. By now, he was scared and more than a little confused, for he did not trust the sounds of the men's voices, or the distant grumbling of the dogs.

Komi continued to coax him in his most per-suasive voice, but Atu refused to cooperate. He lay down in a corner and closed his eyes. Surely this

52

would show his young friend that he was not interested. But the Eskimo boy persisted. He kept beating on the stone wall with a rock, saying urgently, "Tooavit! Tooavit!"

Suddenly, a strange and terrifying thing happened. Leather thongs were whipped around him and he was lifted bodily out of the pen. Once on the ground, though, the thongs were removed and he was free. The sight of him set the dogs to growling and barking. There was so much noise that he dashed down the hill and out of sight before Komi could catch him.

"Eye! Eye! Stop! Stop!," Komi called, but Atu kept on running until he was so far away that he could not hear the sound of the barking dogs or the voice of his little friend. He wandered most of the night, but when the sun spread its warmth over the ice fields he remembered the stone igloo on the hillside and decided to return to the boy.

Next morning, when Komi came out of the igloo, he saw Atu standing at the foot of the hill. He was overjoyed to see the cub, but carefully refrained from running down to greet him. The little bear might run off again. Komi walked until he was close enough to throw his arms around Atu.

Hugging him, he said, "I knew you would come back. You had to come back. We are friends."

Atu rubbed himself against Komi. The caressing tone of voice and the arms around his neck soothed him. He was no longer afraid.

Komi wanted to keep Atu in the igloo at night, but his father objected. Little bears were too mischievous. So Atu slept on top of a tumbled mass of rough ice where a cave-like hollow was filled with snow. It made a snug bed and was high enough to protect him from any dog that might get loose. He looked at the stone pen wistfully, for frozen meat was now heaped on top of the driftwood planks and rocks. He could smell the fat and his mouth juiced. When he stood up by the pen to sniff its contents Komi slapped him. The slap was sharp enough to hurt his feelings, and it taught him a lesson. He was to stay away from the pen.

Atu stayed away, although there were times when he was tempted to disobey, especially when the wind was strong and the odor filled his nostrils with tantalizing pungence. He could look longingly at the friend who was his ally in all things except this one. The pen was taboo.

Atu and Komi played together every day. When Atu's shoulder healed, Komi hitched him to a small sled, one his father had made. Komi wanted Atu to pull him as the dogs pulled the big sledges, but Atu was not too agreeable. Though he sensed

it was only a game, he did not enjoy pulling anything, not even his friend. Each time he was hitched
to the sledge he got tangled in the sealskin lines and
was stubborn about getting untangled. Komi always
thought his antics so amusing that he laughed constantly. His laughter excited Atu to the point of
showing off. He would stand up on his hind feet,
suddenly fall down, roll over and kick as hard as
he could, then jump up and hit his head with his
forepaws. He even tried turning somersaults in the
harness, but then he got so tangled he couldn't
move. This went on day after day. In the evening
both were exhausted—Komi from laughter, Atu
from exercise.

As the days grew longer and warmer, Atu
watched the birds flying overhead. He noticed, too,
that the ice foot was breaking up and melting, forming open water between the ice fields and the shore.
Suddenly he felt restless. Deep down, he sensed that
the endless horizon beyond the ice fields was the
world he had explored with his mother, and he had
a growing urgency to return to it.

Komi noticed the gradual change in Atu and
felt sad. He realized that the cub would not stay
with him much longer, but he had hoped he would
not leave until the end of summer. Each time that
he had watched the little bear cross the ice to open

water, staying longer and longer, he knew the hour of his departure was rapidly approaching. So, one day, when Atu failed to return, Komi was not surprised. He understood. But he was afraid for his friend.

"Be careful when you go hunting, Father," he warned. "Do not shoot Ahtuckta."

Komi's father smiled in return. Of course he would not shoot a young bear, especially one as small as Ahtuckta. But a grown bear, that was different. A man must look after himself first.

CHAPTER 5

Summertime

Atu followed the base of the towering cliffs. Suka-nuk was a shining ball of light in the sky, bathing the Northland with its cheerful warmth. Here and there patches of snow had melted, and he sniffed the bare ground. It smelled good, even though it gave him nothing to eat. He walked until he grew tired, then he curled up on a mossy bank and went to sleep.

When he awoke he felt hungrier than ever. He ate some of the moss, but he did not like it. He wanted seal meat; that stuck to his ribs. But the lack of food did not turn him back to the igloo. He had answered the call of his inheritance; instinct would lead him on.

When he found piles of rocks he stopped and scraped through them, picking them up and banging them together over and over just to hear the noisy "crack-clack" they made. Hearing a loud twittering of birds, he looked up. The sky seemed full of swirling, feathery bodies. He stood watching them for a few minutes, then went on.

As he approached a pile of rocks he saw a big sea goose. It was flopping on the ground, having trouble getting air-borne again. Atu ran forward. When the goose saw him coming it began to honk and flap its wings harder than ever and took off, half-running, half-flying.

Atu pursued it, not because it looked like something to eat, but because the chase promised excitement. Several minutes of lively action followed. When the goose ran, Atu ran, and when the goose tried to fly, he leaped in the air, making scooping motions with his forepaws. With one scoop he accidentally caught a wing, pinning the bird down. He stared at it curiously, wondering what to do with it.

There was no indecision about the frightened, hissing goose. It reached up and pecked viciously at his eyes. Startled, Atu let go. Free again, the goose

58

ran. Angry now, Atu followed it over the rock piles, grabbing at the fleeing bird each time it swished by him. He had not liked being pecked, and he meant to slap the goose hard if he caught it again. But the big bird eluded him by rising in wobbly flight to a cliff shelf out of his reach, where it honked derisively at him. Atu stared upward, growling in answer. Could he have eaten the bird? If so, his warm meal had flown away.

He padded around rather aimlessly after that, then headed for a lead. He had not gone far when he heard sounds that he recognized. Had Eskimo dogs found his trail?

His heart beat faster. If the men in the igloo were searching for him they must not find him. He did not want to return. Streaking across the ice, he swam the lead and hid in a low pressure ridge. There he stood sniffing the air until he could no longer catch the scent of the dogs.

He was in no hurry to leave the safety of his hiding place. It was hours before he made his way onto a level stretch of ice where he found pools of water just deep enough to wade in. He splashed around playfully for several minutes until he saw the carcass of a Metik, or eider duck, lying beside another pool. He ran over and examined it carefully. Though feathers covered the body he was hungry enough to eat anything. So he ate the duck. The feathers caught in his mouth, the downy ones sticking to his tongue. He pawed at them until his mouth was free, then he scratched at the ring of fluffy white feathers around his black-tipped nose and sneezed. They tickled. He had not really enjoyed his meal, but the bird was better than nothing.

Atu stood on his hind feet and tested the warm breeze, wondering if he could catch a seal all by himself. He could try. As he trotted off across the bay ice he did not feel too confident, but he intended to do what his mother had taught him.

The day was warm and sunny, so it was not long before he caught the odor of seal. Though the Atluk was too far away to see, his nose followed the smell guide until he found it. But he had arrived too late. A mother bear and her two cubs were already feasting on the seal, smacking loudly as they chewed on the warm blubber.

Delighted that he was no longer alone, Atu ran over to the mother bear. Surely she would share this game with him. Instead, she turned swiftly and slapped his small rump a stinging blow. This was to let him know that he must not come near while they were eating.

Atu watched the cubs while they ate, envying every mouthful they swallowed. He was so hungry that his mouth juiced and his empty belly made rumbling noises. If only he could manage to slip one small piece of blubber away.

But the mother bear controlled the dinner. The seal lay directly between her huge paws. There was nothing he could do.

Later, she stopped eating long enough to look him over carefully, then she glanced around, sniffing, as if trying to pick up the scent of another bear. She must have decided that he was alone for she suddenly tossed him a chunk of blubber.

He swallowed it whole. Hoping for more, he made grunt-like whines, and the mother bear threw him another piece. But before he could pick it up one of her own cubs snatched it away. Quick as a flash she slapped her youngster, retrieved the blubber and gave it back to him. He swallowed the second piece whole, too, afterward smacking as noisily as the other cubs. Now his belly was not grumbling so loudly.

The young bears continued to chew noisily. Atu growled to draw attention to himself again, but this time the mother bear only looked at him and bared her long yellow teeth. It seemed she was through feeding him.

Atu went to one side and sat down. Though his belly felt much better, there was room in it for more food. He did not want to leave the mother bear even though she had slapped him. He decided to wait and follow her.

When the other cubs finished eating their mother drew them close and let them nurse. Atu wanted to be cuddled, to be held against her breast, too, the way his own mother had held him. He moved closer, his bright eyes begging hopefully. But the big white bear paid no attention to him. He moved even closer, and she growled and bared her teeth.

Atu backed up hastily, afraid of her.

The longer the cubs nursed and smacked, the more restless he became. He had never missed his mother more than at this moment. He made sob-like grunts, his round little belly jerking with the force of his emotion, but his unhappiness failed to impress the mother bear. Pushing her cubs away, she got up and ambled toward a few outlying islands across the bay.

Atu followed. He did not know if she would resent his presence, but he intended to stay far enough behind so she would not take offense.

The mother bear chose the largest of the islands where the hillsides were covered with tall grass and sprinkled with white, yellow and purple flowers, even though banks of snow still lay on the ground.

Other hillsides were covered with soft moss in shades of green and red with tiny pink blossoms no larger than the head of a pin. A brook wound through the grass with rushing sounds, as if anxious to tumble over a little cliff beyond. The stream was full of lively fish of all sizes, darting through the sparkling water like silvery shadows. Atu was so excited that he jumped into the water and grabbed at the fish. The cubs were doing the same thing, only they were eating them, so he scooped up one and ate it. He had never tasted fish before, but quickly decided that the slippery wrigglers were delicious. Every time he caught one he ate it, and it wasn't long before he had a satisfying meal. After that, he sloshed up and down the narrow stream, fish darting between his short legs. He was so amused by what he was doing that he forgot about the other bears. When he remembered to look for them, they had gone away.

At first he thought he would find the mother bear, but the stream was so full of fish he did not want to leave. Here food was easy to catch. He would stay.

He continued to catch and eat fish until his belly was uncomfortably full. Then he went to sleep on a grassy hillside and he slept a long, long time.

Next day, when he returned to the stream, he

63

found a different mother bear and her two cubs. They were young he-bears like himself. The three bears stared at each other, then Atu waded into the stream. The brother cubs came over and watched as he caught several fish. They acted as if they wanted to be friendly. But Atu was cautious. Though they looked friendly, their mother was watching from upstream. He did not trust her. She might slap him if he played with her cubs.

Suddenly one of the cubs picked up a rock and tossed it at him. The other cub opened his mouth and stuck out his tongue, as if he thought his brother was very amusing. Then both of them ran. Atu refused to chase them. It might be a trap.

He waited until they returned and began to throw rocks in his direction again, then he stomped his forefeet and jumped at them. The brother cubs accepted this as an invitation to become better acquainted and trotted over to him. Their little black-tipped noses touched his and the three of them sniffed each other timidly, then they whirled and ran round and round, chasing each other in a lively game.

The mother bear left the stream and made her way up a hill. Once she stopped, glanced back at her cubs, and growled. They hurried after her. Atu did not want to lose his new friends and followed them.

When the mother bear reached the top of the hill, Atu saw her sniff through piles of rocks and wondered what she was looking for. It was even more exciting when she began to dig in the ground. Her sharp claws made the dirt fly. Though her body appeared to be heavy, her movements were lithe and quick. She kept hunting until she found some queer things that were round and smooth—bird's eggs. After rolling them carefully in her huge paws, she put them in her mouth, spitting out the shells afterwards. Then she smacked and smacked, as if the eggs tasted better than fish.

Atu selected a narrow, rocky ledge far enough away so she could not reach out and slap him, and crept along cautiously. He found several nests. They were formed of grass and dry seaweed, the five little eggs inside protected only by layers of soft down which the female bird had plucked from her breast. Atu ate all of the eggs he could find. Soon his face was dripping with yolks. His black tongue licked as far up as it could reach, then he flipped it in and out of his mouth, smacking with pleasure.

The mother bear watched him with a surly expression. If she was thinking about chasing him away she evidently changed her mind, for she returned to the valley floor, grunting all the way down the hill.

66

When Atu could not find any more eggs, he joined the mother bear and her cubs. It seemed she had a new interest. This time she was digging for sweet-tasting roots. Soon all of them were doing the same thing. The roots were not big, but they were good to eat, and the next few days were spent hunting and digging for them. In between times, they fished in the tundra stream and slept in the warm sun, relaxed and happy.

It seemed that the mother bear never stayed in one place very long. In a few days she was on the move again, leading her cubs across the rough island hills to Smith Sound, then along the coast to Kane Basin. Atu wasn't sure he should go with them. So far, the mother bear had not objected to his presence, but if she sensed he was trying to join them permanently, she might chase him away. After so much happy companionship, he did not want to be left behind. Perhaps if he did not follow too closely she would not be angry.

As he neared the crest of a hill he could see the mother bear and her cubs making their way down the opposite slope, headed for a rocky beach. She stopped and looked back at him, as if undecided what to do about him, then she went on. She did not appear to be angry, so he followed.

As he stared at the endless horizon of shining

67

ice, checked and sliced with ragged spears of green, sunlit water, he grew more and more excited. Now and then the sound of booming split the silence as ice broke up under the heat of Sukanuk. Atu's friends were already swimming in the water, so he hurried down the hillside to the rocky beach. At first the sea looked deep and scary, and he hesitated, but he took a deep breath and plunged in, landing with a big belly-flop. He swam along easily, his black-tipped nose a dark blob against the green-colored water, his body tingling with its icy coldness. Wisps of fog drifted across the sky, hanging down in thin curtains of salty freshness.

Suddenly a deep sense of belonging filled him with confidence. This was not a lead, but the sea itself.

Shaking his head, he rolled over and over, puffing and blowing. At last he had found his real home.

CHAPTER 6

New Adventures

The summer was short, barely three months in northern Greenland, then the days began to darken. Atu stayed with the mother bear and her two cubs. She would not let him come near her, but she never failed to feed him when she caught a seal.

The three cubs played together all day long. They never seemed to get tired. The only time Atu felt lonely was when the mother bear cuddled her little ones. He would sit to one side and bawl, hoping to draw attention to himself, but after a while he was forced to accept the fact that she considered him an outsider.

In September, the birds began to fly south, indicating that winter was barely a month away. When the sea had been quiet for a few days the surface of the water began to solidify and take on a greasy appearance, the first sign of freezing.

In October, Sukanuk dipped low behind the horizon, and the gray Arctic twilight gradually gave way to the dark blackness that prevailed day and night. Occasionally big stars twinkled overhead, and the Aurora Borealis waved its glowing veil of ever-changing colors of red, yellow and green across the sky. The ice, now hard, was an endless field of white, trackless and inhospitable.

Atu grew used to the darkness and the blizzards. When the storms raged, the mother bear holed up in some sheltered spot with her cubs beside her, but he had to find his own protective niche. He learned to curl up under a huge snow drift, or low hummock, where the freezing winds could not blow directly on him. Sometimes he overslept, and when this happened he was left behind. He knew the odor of the other bears, so he sniffed until he caught it, then he hurried to catch up with them.

One day was like another, dark, with icy winds

blowing straight down from the North Pole bringing heavy snowstorms. The mother bear was constantly on the move. Her keen sense of smell kept them from starving. She knew that during winter, seals keep breathing holes open in the deep ice by industriously scratching and gnawing. The first time she caught a seal under the ice Atu was excited. He and the two cubs watched as she sniffed around a globe-shaped hollow of snow directly above a hole. The narrow opening inside was covered with a thin crust of ice. The mother bear gave Atu and her cubs a warning glance. They understood, for they too could smell the seal. As they sat staring intently at the hole, not daring to move, the seal suddenly popped up for a breath of air. Quick as a flash the mother bear hooked her claws into its foreflippers and pulled it out of the hole. In a few moments they had a warm meal. Although the mother bear always fed him, Atu felt he never had enough to eat. Several times when he was left alone he found dead birds and ate them, or hunted along ice cracks, digging out tiny frozen shrimps and mollusks. But he could never find enough to take the edge from his hunger.

As Atu and his friends made their way through the long, dark days and nights of the Arctic winter, time meant nothing to them. It was in February, the month that marked the gradual returning of Sukanuk, that Atu sensed a change in the weather. Fingers of gray light spread across the horizon, and though they did not stay long, he felt a deep stirring within him. It would not be long until seals would be lying on the ice again, warm meals for hungry bears. Soon there would be plenty of game to fill their empty bellies.

About the middle of March, Sukanuk appeared higher in the sky. From then on until May the weather was a combination of daylight and cloudiness. As usual, a few open leads were between the floes, and Nauya, the graceful glaucous gull of the Far North, was flying along the shoreline.

Atu was now more than a year old and beginning to feel quite independent. He no longer minded the mother bear and her cubs leaving him behind, and gradually he felt little need of their company. One day he even grew bold enough to challenge the mother bear over a seal, getting soundly cuffed for his impertinence. He lost interest in the bears after that, thus bringing their once-happy companionship to an abrupt end.

But finding game alone was not as easy as he had expected. Long before Sukanuk was warm enough to draw seals to the top of the ice he was following little blue and white foxes, fighting over

72

blubber left by other bears. As the noses of the little foxes were as sensitive to odors as his, he often arrived too late. When this happened he growled and shook himself angrily, even pounding the ice with his forepaws. Losing any part of a meal, no matter how small, was enough to throw him into a temper. Once he found a band of Ookuda and chased them, thinking he might catch an Arctic hare. But they outdistanced him rapidly. He went on his way again, grunting with vexation.

During the month of April he first saw herds of walrus going north for the summer. What enormous creatures they were—their "ooching" could be heard miles away. But he was not interested in Awick. They were too big for him to kill.

In June great flocks of birds came flying back from the south. Atu sensed it was time to search for Netsik, the little ringed seals. Soon they would be lying on the ice, basking in the sunshine, always with a watchful eye for their enemy, the ice bear.

When Atu reached the edge of a floe, he saw a glistening ice pan not too far away. It was round and smooth and just his size. He swam out to it and lay down. As he looked at Sukanuk and the shining ice, he began to feel drowsy. He curled up, and in a few minutes was fast asleep.

While he slept the ice pan drifted with the cur-

73

rent. It turned round and round, and the drowsy motion lulled him into even deeper sleep. It was a long time before he awoke, and when he did he had no idea where he was. But he was not afraid. The sea was his home. Closing his eyes, he went back to sleep. The next time he awoke, Sukanuk was shining even more brightly, and the ice pan was bumping and grinding against a larger one. As usual, he was hungry.

He sniffed the warm air. Tahtara, the kittiwake gulls, were flying overhead. Now and then they swooped downward, as if searching for something to eat on the ice. Though they were only birds, their presence gave him a feeling of companionship.

Slipping into the water, Atu struck off across the sea. Floes of all sizes dotted the horizon. In comparison, his white head looked like a blob of ice as it bobbed up and down in the green water. He felt almost lost among the cold islands, but he kept swimming, only rising up to peer and sniff.

One time he saw a strange animal in the water and wondered what it was. The unfamiliar object was Kalilewuk, the narwhal, long and grayish-white, mottled with black, and with a tusk, or ivory horn, protruding out of its jaw. Atu thought it was a strange-looking creature. He had seen nothing like it before.

74

Climbing hurriedly onto the nearest floe, Atu watched with fascination as the 2,000-pound whale cut a wide, billowing path in the sea. It swam by him with a great swishing noise, making a shrill whistling sound each time it lifted its snout out of the water, at the same time exhaling a vapor-like substance that looked like a cloud of mist through its blowhole.

Atu watched it with a mixture of curiosity and fear. He wanted it to go away because he was hungry, but he was afraid to get in the water while it was cruising around. Though his belly was making growling noises from hunger, he decided the safest thing to do was to stay on the floe.

Kalilewuk seemed in no hurry to leave. It skimmed through the water, now and then rising up to spout its steam and blow its whistle. Atu paced back and forth, back and forth, growing more and more impatient with his unwelcome visitor. Surely this creature would go away before too long, then he could hunt for his dinner.

He had no sooner sat down on the floe, prepared to outwait the strange monster, when it suddenly submerged. At last it was gone. Now for his dinner!

As he stood silhouetted against the sky, many different odors came to him on the warm air. All of them smelled interesting, but when he caught the pungent odor of seal, he slipped into the water and followed the smell guide until he found it.

Instead of one seal as he had expected, he found a herd. They were Ookjuk, bearded seals, much larger than Netsik. Atu watched their lazy movements. The herd was noisy, making "awking" sounds.

Atu's body sank deeper in the water. Only his eyes and ears and black-tipped nose were visible. He swam around for several minutes, planning a method of attack. If they saw him, or smelled him, they would jump quickly into the water and swim away. He sensed he was no match for them in the water. They were too fast.

If he kept behind the ridge-side of the floe the wind was in his favor, and his furry body could not be seen. As he floated along like a blob of ice, he saw a young seal lying near the floe rim. It was just the right size to handle.

He maneuvered his body slowly until he was close enough to throw himself upward, then he pounced. Clutching the young seal firmly between his jaws, he dragged it into the water and swam away, intending to reach a nearby floe before the other seals were aware of what had happened.

Instead, his quarry made such a racket that the

entire herd piled into the water at once and pursued him. As their darting, rolling bodies threshed the water around him, they bit him with their sharp teeth.

Atu had not expected this and fought back, two hundred pounds of angry striking force behind his sharp claws. But this was not enough. His movements were hampered by the heavy body of the seal pup which was making strenuous efforts to escape.

Frightened at the unexpected sharpness of the seals' teeth, he dropped the pup. As soon as he let go he was allowed to go on his way. Crawling out of the water, he shook himself and sat down, his face and body stinging. Angry and disappointed, he wondered what to do next. He was still hungry. His first effort had been woefully unsuccessful. He must keep on trying.

As he sat looking around rather forlornly, he was more than ever aware that he must eat plenty of blubber in order to put on fat for the coming winter, the winter that would be long and harsh, with too little food. Soon Netsik would be under the snow and ice, hard to find, and even harder to dig out.

Once again he began his wanderings, crossing floe after floe, stopping to stand on his hind feet and scent the air. He was so engrossed in checking the

78

various scents that at first he did not notice a boat coming toward him through the ice-dotted sea. Not until the sound of its motor reached him did he look around. What could this strange chugging thing be? He stood watching it with growing interest until he suddenly caught the odor of man. Then he fled in terror.

Hunters climbed on the floe, while their Eskimo guide steered their boat along the ice rim.

Atu glanced back quickly and saw the men pursuing him. The floe was too small to hide on, so he took to the water. Ropes began to swing at him from several directions, but he managed to elude them. With short legs churning, he swam to a jagged mass of ice a short distance away. He was pulling himself up the steep rim when he felt something flick lightly against the back of his neck. He shook his head so violently that he almost fell back in the water, but whatever it was slipped off, leaving him free to streak across the rough ice.

The Eskimo in the boat watched Atu disappear, a smile on his lips. Later, when he returned to pick up his companions, his answer to their query—"What happened?"—was laconic. "Ice was too rough to hunt," he said. "Too many water pools on the other side of the floe. The cub got away."

Although the men were disappointed, they decided to give up the hunt. Perhaps they would find another cub to take back with them. The Eskimo sat quietly in the stern of the boat. How glad he was that he had seen the long, ragged scar on the cub's right shoulder! These men need not know why the rope had only lightly touched the young bear's neck. That would be his secret. How proud Komi would be when he told him that he had saved little Ahtuckta from being captured and taken far from his home in the Arctic.

CHAPTER 7

Purple Shadows

Atu continued from one floe to another until he felt
it was safe to stop, then he stood on his hind feet
and tested the wind in all directions. He could no
longer catch the odor of man, man whom he had
forgotten in this new world of adventure, nor
could he hear or see the chugging object skimming
across the water. It was all very confusing and fright-
ening, a reminder that he must be more watchful.

A sense of relief finally quieted the chills of
fear, and he sniffed exploringly, hunger once again
gnawing at his belly. If he followed the foxes he
knew he would find scraps, but he wanted a seal

81

for himself, one he could gorge on, filling his empty belly until no more blubber could be stuffed in.

Once again he started across the ice, swinging his head from side to side, scenting the air as he walked. When he finally caught the odor of seal he found it lying by its Atluk near the edge of the floe.

Atu was puzzled. The ice was smooth, and the seal was so near the water it could jump in and swim away before he could catch it. His prey had a decided advantage over him. He must outwit it in some way.

Slipping into the water he swam along easily, only stopping to rise up and scent the air, careful to keep his body odor downwind to the seal, for a seal can smell a bear as easily as a bear can smell a seal. He was so quiet that the water hardly rippled around his shoulders. It took him several minutes to reach the Atluk. Taking a deep breath, he suddenly dived under the ice and swam to the blowhole, scratching on it with his sharp claws.

The sound evidently attracted the seal, for down it plunged, right into his waiting jaws. But it was so much heavier than he had expected that the force of its weight pushed him even deeper into the sea, breaking his hold. He rolled over and over before he could right himself, then he shot to the surface, looking for his quarry. It was gone!

82

He crawled out of the water in a real temper. Picking up chunks of ice, he threw them about, slapping everything around him. It wasn't long, though, before he caught the odor of seal again and his anger quickly cooled. This time the scent came from the opposite side of the floe.

He moved cautiously toward the Atluk. Here the ice was rough, with depressions deep enough to hide in.

When he was within a few feet of his quarry he peeked carefully above an ice bump. The seal was lying on its side. Atu could almost taste the blubber in his mouth, warm and juicy, filling him with strength and lining his ribs with fat for the coming winter. He must not lose this game.

Turning his black-tipped claws under and covering his dark blob of a nose with them, he inched his way over the ice. He hardly breathed, so intent was he on his prey. Impatience gave way to patience, the patience his mother had taught him.

He inched his way forward slowly. It seemed a long time before he was near enough to pounce on the seal.

Quickly grabbing it by its hind flippers, he pulled it to him and sank his sharp teeth into its neck. In a few seconds he had a warm meal. Rising up, he looked around and growled. He was no longer a cub to eat with foxes, fighting them for scraps. He was strong now, able to make his own kills, entirely independent.

Atu ate all of the seal. The fat was rich, so rich that he felt slightly ill afterwards. But he did not seek the grass on the island hills to soothe his belly. Though he was uncomfortable, he hunted a nice spot in the sun and curled up among chunks of ice. Here he went to sleep.

When he awoke he was again a tireless hunter, crisscrossing the bays and inlets, working his way along the Greenland coast north, eating all of the game he could find, fattening himself for the long Arctic winter ahead.

One day, he met several ice bears. There were two mothers and four cubs, and two big males. The males reminded him of Boc, and he wanted to go over to them, but they looked so surly he was not sure he should be friendly.

He stood watching them from a distance until the cubs came over, one by one, and sniffed him timidly. A playful slap followed. This seemed to be the signal for all of them to join in the game of "getting acquainted" and they began to bump and chase him.

Atu was delighted. He rolled and tumbled and bumped them, too. When he saw one cub near the

84

ice rim he slipped up behind her and pushed her in. The others piled on him and tried to duck him. A lively scramble followed as the five young bears wrestled each other.

Day after day, Atu and his friends chased big silver-looking fish in the sea, ducked each other, or swam to some iceberg where they climbed as high as they could, then leaped off into space, landing in the water with a terrific splash. Down, down, down they went, rising to the top again with a great puffing and blowing.

The warm, happy days passed so quickly that Atu was hardly aware winter was upon them until cold, sharp winds and the darkened sky brought flurries of snow drifting across the ice. Later the storms grew so heavy that the mother bears and their cubs started south, while the males wandered off by themselves. Atu wanted to go with them, but when he followed, they drew back their lips and growled. It was plain they did not want to be bothered with a stray cub.

The shore waters were now frozen. The pack ice which had broken up and drifted with the wind and tide all summer was frozen solidly for hundreds of miles. Once more the Northland was held in the vise-like grip of the long Arctic winter.

Atu was not afraid to be alone, but after so

much friendly companionship he felt lonely. Though he had a heavy layer of fat on his ribs this did not mean he could hole up for the winter. He sensed that he must seek game constantly or his body would soon be lean and he would starve.

When January came, he was two years old and weighed nearly three hundred pounds. As he walked through his world of purple shadows his step was firm and proud. Sniffing the cold, almost brittle air, he stopped to investigate snow mounds and low hummocks, always hoping to catch the odor of seal. Following behind Atu were several foxes. They kept darting across his path and peeking at him from behind snow drifts. They were waiting for blubber.

Game was hard to find. Even now, several days had passed since his last meal. His belly felt lean and his disposition was surly. He had learned long ago that only the strong survived, an instinct that kept him sniffing and digging, sniffing and digging.

A big white Arctic wolf slipped along behind him, as if wondering whether the bear was young enough to frighten easily, in case it caught a seal. There was one way to find out.

Atu finally uncovered an Atluk and hooked out a seal as the mother bear had done. As he sank his teeth into the warm blubber, the wolf glided swiftly across the ice and leaped on his back, its long fangs tearing at his neck. Roaring with pain and anger, Atu whirled and twisted his body with such a quick, powerful motion that the wolf flew into the air, spitting white fur. When it landed on the ice Atu was there to meet it. He hit it a glancing blow that drew blood, and it rolled over and over, but came at him again, fangs bared, growling with rage. This time Atu's claws ripped its side. Howling, the wolf leaped backwards, its eyes filled with a murderous gleam. Atu roared and charged again, ready to kill this enemy, but the wolf was through fighting. It had misjudged the size and temper of the young bear. Dripping blood, the wolf wheeled and ran.

Atu had not known there was an enemy like the wolf in his world. As he watched it disappear into the gloom his emotions were a mixture of fury and disbelief. His neck pained him where the long fangs had struck and he shook his head. Growling, he tore at the blubber, afterwards sucking the remaining bits into his mouth quickly and smacking. It was a small meal, hardly enough to fill his belly. He must have more game.

To this end memory served him. He would return to the stone pen on the hillside. As he padded along his warm breath vapored. Ice crystals sparkled against his white fur. Stars pinpointed the sky, and Ahningahnah, the moon, which hung like a great silver ball, turned the night into a veritable fairyland.

Hurrying on, Atu's hairy-padded feet walked the long icy miles with confidence and expectancy. When he neared the hills where the snow was deeper, he walked along the ice foot, the great dark cliffs frowning down on him like angry giants.

Approaching his destination, he grew more and more eager and excited. Inside the pen would be game, plenty of game for a hungry bear.

At first, only one thought was dominant—he must fill his empty belly. But as he stood looking up at the familiar hillside, he suddenly remembered the boy with the soft voice and kind hands. He was tempted to walk directly to the igloo as he had done in the past, but instinct warned him against this. Now that he was here he began to feel uneasy.

He stood sniffing the air carefully. The wind was coming directly toward him, so he caught the odor of the dogs, though he could not see them. He knew they would be curled up on the snow, heads tucked under bushy tails, fast asleep. With the breeze in his favor he could circle the top of the igloo and approach the pen from the opposite side. He would slip in, get the frozen meat, and depart at once.

As he circled the dogs no sense of real danger

stirred within him, for there were no unpleasant memories about this place. If time and experience had not changed him, he would have gone up to the igloo and let his presence be known. But he had become a creature of the wild. He could not return to what he had outgrown.

When Atu reached the pen he found that it was covered. Rocks and boards were piled high. In order to reach the meat he must push these aside.

Standing on his hind feet he hooked his claws between the boards. Then he pulled himself upwards, his muscles bulging and rippling under the strain. One free forearm pushed at the heavy coverings, but they refused to move. He kept on pushing, hunger and impatience urging him on. With food almost within his grasp he did not intend to give up.

When his efforts still remained unsuccessful, anger mounted. Summoning every ounce of strength he possessed, he gave a mighty shove, dislodging a rock. It tumbled off the boards and rolled down the hillside, making a loud clatter.

The crash alerted the dogs. Jumping up, they barked excitedly. And when they saw Atu they made such a racket that Komi and his father crawled through the Toksuk, guns in hand. Through the purple shadows of the night, the father could see the outline of a bear. His first thought was to shoot. The walrus and seal meat was their very life. He must protect it at all costs.

Getting quickly to his feet he sighted the gun. As his finger squeezed the trigger, a hand pushed the barrel violently upward. The bullet missed. Atu escaped unharmed.

Komi's father whirled on him, shouting angrily, "Why did you do that!"

"It was Ahtuckta!" Komi replied excitedly.

"Ahtuckta! Ahtuckta! Every cub you see is Ahtuckta! How could you tell in the dark? *I* could not! Besides, the bear was after our winter supply of meat. I would kill even Ahtuckta to protect that, and you know it."

"*I* know it," Komi replied sadly, "but Ahtuckta does not. Perhaps he was starving, Father, and remembered we had once fed him."

His father grunted in disbelief. "How could he remember us? He has been gone too long. You are forgetting that when the wind is right *any* bear can smell the meat. This stray must have scented it while walking along the ice foot."

Komi did not answer. Perhaps his father was right. But he could also be mistaken. Somehow, Komi felt sure that the bear they had seen had been Ahtuckta.

90

"I just *know* it," he said to himself. But the thought brought little comfort. His father would have killed Ahtuckta just the same.

Atu ran faster than he had in a long time. When he sensed he was not being pursued he stopped running. He had recognized the rifle shot for what it was, and a strange feeling of loneliness came over him. With the sharp crack of the rifle the last human tie was broken.

Glancing quickly over his shoulder he sniffed, then turned and went on again, a tireless wanderer searching for game.

CHAPTER 8

The Rogue Bear

Atu had not gone far when he met a young bear, a she-bear, not as old as he. When she saw him she seemed delighted, and ran over and sniffed him shyly.

Atu backed up, growling. Where was the cub's mother? He scented the air, but he did not catch the odor of another bear.

Anxious to get rid of this female cub he growled even louder, looking as surly as he knew how. But the cub was not impressed. She kept running up to him, then leaping aside, as if she expected him to cuff her. But her eyes held no fear.

Hoping to discourage her, he slapped at her, then he ran. It was an undignified retreat, but he meant to get rid of her quickly. Although his long legs carried him at a fast pace, the young female was right at his heels. It seemed she intended to join him whether he liked it or not. So he quit running. He could see there was no use. She meant to follow wherever he went. Whirling, he roared out his growls, trying to frighten her. But she just looked back at him, bright-eyed, as if she thought he was playing some kind of game.

Now Atu was uncertain what to do. Perhaps nothing short of a hard slap would meet the problem, but he did not want to hit her. Finally he decided to ignore her. This was hard to do for she kept running around him, jumping at him playfully. She seemed overjoyed with his company and evidently expected him to feel the same way about her.

Atu's patience was at an end. He raised one forepaw, intending to slap her hard enough to discourage her. But when he looked closely at Tonda, she was so sweet, so trusting, he could not hit her. Slowly drawing back his paw, Atu growled low, hesitated, then turned away. He was defeated. Tonda stared at him for a few moments, then suddenly ran

94

over and slurped his face. She knew she had been accepted even though this young male was not too agreeable.

Hours later, when no mother bear put in an appearance, Atu understood that Tonda was alone like himself, and the strange loneliness he had felt left him. Though hunger gnawed at his belly, he was content. He would look after this she-cub, feed her, protect her. Now he had a companion.

As they walked along, snow blew in clouds across the ice. The white fields were broken here and there by pressure ridges, and by icebergs frozen into the mass. Despite their hunger the young bears romped tirelessly. Atu was careful not to hurt Tonda, she was so much smaller than he. But she was not careful. She was rough, acting as if she were still playing with her mother. Sometimes she raked her claws across his face, drawing blood. When this happened he raised his paws in a threatening manner, but he never hit her. As she ran around him, leaping and slapping at him, her eyes were filled with mischief. She did not expect him to hurt her. He was her protector and friend.

When February, or "twilight" time in the Arctic, began to pass, Sukanuk rose higher in the sky. The cold was still intense, the wind terrible, but Atu and Tonda, in their oily white fur, never minded the freezing winds or blinding snowstorms. They were always hungry, for seals were far apart, and they crossed the barren ice fields constantly, looking for game. On warmer days they lay on the snow-covered ice and rolled and stretched. Atu loved to scratch himself. He would stand up by some jagged piece of ice and grunt with pleasure as he took turns rubbing his back, then his belly. Tonda imitated him. She would find a spot to her liking and scratch herself as industriously as he.

Although the bitter cold of winter was slowly passing, heavy fog drifted in and spread across the ice fields like a thick curtain. Sometimes it hung in long, heavy fingers of mist for several days; then, like a giant broom, the wind would sweep it away, and Sukanuk would warm the air again.

One day the wind carried the pungent odor of whale to the bears. Atu did not know it was Kalil-ewuk, but he sensed it was game of some kind. He and Tonda followed the scent for miles until they came to a channel of water that separated them from a rocky beach. Here the snow was newly melted and they found birds, bears and foxes gathered together around the carcass of a whale.

They swam the channel and quickly joined in the free meal. Other bears were feeding, too intent on their dinner to be annoyed by the newcomers.

Birds and foxes snatched tidbits, ever-watchful for slapping paws. Here was a feast to which all were invited, and the guests were making the most of their unexpected banquet.

Atu and Tonda secured some of the blubber and retired to eat it. When Atu finished eating he looked around. The friendly cubs which had dived with him from the iceberg were feasting too. They came over to Atu and sniffed Tonda with interest, but they were too sleepy to play. They walked away and lay down. Atu saw the mother bear and the brother cubs too. They were big like him, and their mother kept slapping at them as if she wanted them to leave her alone. It was plain that she was no longer interested in her cubs, for now they were old enough to take care of themselves.

With his belly stuffed, and feeling pleasantly uncomfortable, Atu grew drowsier by the moment and started up the hill intending to take a nap. As he passed Tonda he bunted her, which meant she was to follow him. But she refused. She was playing with another she-cub and did not want to be ordered about.

Atu was slightly annoyed by her behavior and wondered if he should force her to go. While trying to decide his next move, he saw a big bear with long, shaggy yellowish-white fur approaching from the opposite direction. He was walking slowly along the rocky beach, glaring at the other bears as if he dared them to stop him from joining the feast. Scars covered his head, showing that he had been a fighter all his life. He opened his mouth as if he meant to roar out defiance at everything around him. Instead, only his black tongue flipped in and out, exposing yellowed and broken teeth. Atu sensed that here was a "rogue" bear, too old to do much hunting for himself, but still strong enough to take game away from younger bears, and mean enough to kill them if they objected. Only the older, stronger bears seemed unafraid of Wonchonka.

Atu watched the old bear as he made his way toward the carcass of the whale, growling. Foxes and young bears scattered as he walked by. But Tonda did not see him. She was too busy playing. As she raced by she bumped into him. Whirling, he slapped at her, sending her rolling. His sharp claws had raked her. She jumped to her feet, howling with pain.

Atu raced down the hillside, caught the old bear and ripped into his flank before Wonchonka could protect himself.

Furious, Wonchonka whirled to fight, but something about the way the other bears were staring at him seemed to change his mind. Small eyes burning with anger, he turned and padded inside the carcass of the whale, making grumbling noises.

Atu licked Tonda's shoulder, then they went higher up the hill and lay down. The tenseness was past. All that could be heard was the chattering of birds, the yipping of foxes and the contented grumbling of the other bears.

Atu relaxed and dropped off to sleep. Sukanuk was so warm that he slept soundly for several hours. Toward evening he awoke, only to find that Tonda had wandered off while he had been sleeping. Wonchonka was gone, too. Fear struck him.

Swimming the channel, he hurried off across the ice fields. As he padded southward his nose sniffed constantly. He swam another lead and pulled himself onto the rough ice, shaking his fur until the water rained down in noisy cascades. Afterward he stood quietly for a few moments, testing the various odors in the air, then he went on.

Intent on finding his small friend, he failed to notice a wide stretch of new ice directly ahead of him. He was on it before he realized that he could not turn back. Flattening himself, he extended his legs for balance, inching his way forward slowly, almost with a swimming motion, the rubbery ice bending under the weight of his heavy body.

Unable to get traction, Atu wasted several minutes of precious time before he reached the hard ice. Belly flat, he dug his claws into it, pulled himself up and hurried on.

He found Tonda in their old hunting grounds eating a seal. But she was not alone. Wonchonka was stalking her.

Atu saw Tonda look up as Wonchonka roared out a challenge.

Instead of retreating, she seemed to crouch even closer to the seal, as if trying to hide behind it.

Atu ran swiftly toward them, for now the old rogue bear, yellow fangs bared, was ready to charge her.

Atu struck from behind. It was a terrific blow, toppling Wonchonka forward. The old bear was surprised. But he sprang to his feet again, charging Atu furiously, eyes glinting red, mouth open, sweeping his huge forearms in a vicious circle. He would kill the young upstart!

Atu easily sidestepped the ripping claws.

Wonchonka roared again, running forward, trying to catch Atu, but when he ran past Tonda she leaped aside and struck him on his flank, her sharp claws drawing blood.

The older bear skidded to a stop, wheeled and slapped at her, but when he felt a searing burn on his right flank, he whirled in the opposite direction.

Atu's claws had ripped into his flesh. Letting out an ear-splitting roar he swung at Atu, but missed.

Atu and Tonda kept dodging easily until the old rogue stopped chasing them and stood still, breathing hard and glowering. He acted as if he did not know what course to pursue. Finally he shook his head, raised up on his hind feet, turned around twice, and collapsed.

Atu and Tonda stared at him in surprise.

Atu felt suspicious. He circled Wonchonka several times, sensing that he was shamming.

But evidently Tonda did not. Before Atu could warn her she trotted over to the prostrate animal and sniffed his body.

Instantly the old bear lashed out at her, but missed, only because his sight was poor. It would have been a killing blow.

Atu and Tonda raced off to a safe distance and stood watching as their enemy got slowly to his feet.

The old bear stared at them for a few minutes, eyes fixed in hatred and frustration, then he limped away.

Atu and Tonda waited until he was out of sight, then they ate what was left of the seal. Afterwards, they eyed each other sleepily. Feeling at peace with his world again, Atu curled up beside his playmate, snuggling one forepaw against her neck. Leaning over, he licked her face. She returned his caress lazily, hunching herself closer to him. Both yawned, closed their eyes and dropped off to sleep.

But for Atu it was a restless sleep. He could not forget the old bear. Perhaps he might return. Several times when he opened his eyes he saw little foxes looking for scraps of blubber. At first he thought he would chase them away, but he felt too lazy. He growled low, which was enough to make them scatter, but not enough to frighten them into leaving. They waited patiently for him to close his eyes again, then slipped back to pick up a few morsels of fat. Afterwards they trotted off, their white bodies blending so perfectly with the snow that they were soon lost to view.

CHAPTER 9

Parting of the Ways

The wind came up and the sky darkened. Soon it was snowing, as if the first bright promise of spring must be dulled by one last jealous touch of winter.

Atu led the way, Tonda by his side. As they followed the ice foot north, they wrestled and chased each other tirelessly. Far out on the ice they heard a loud roaring of walrus. Awick was returning to the Northland for the summer. Several hours later, the snow stopped falling. Crystal flakes on their fur sparkled in the sunlight, but under the warmer rays of Sukanuk the snowflakes began to melt in shiny little trickles.

104

Rounding a rocky point the bears saw Eskimos and dog teams coming toward them. Whirling, Atu and Tonda ran. But not soon enough. Rifle shots pierced the silence and bullets began zinging against the snow-covered ice, spattering them with fine crystal chunks.

Again came the crack of a rifle. This time a bullet tore into Atu's right shoulder, burying itself in the muscles. The force of the blow knocked him over and he rolled into a crevice. Terrified, Tonda ran, but when Atu did not follow she returned to where he lay sprawled on the ice. She nudged him urgently. He must get up.

The raw wound burned and Atu bit at his shoulder, then he got up slowly, painfully, and limped away, blood trailing after him. The sight of the blood spurred him on to even greater efforts of escape. The two of them crossed a plateau that led for several miles above the ice foot, but Atu sensed this was dangerous. His human enemies could track him here.

Changing his course he followed another range of rough, icy plateaus, finally disappearing into an underground crevice. At last he felt safe. Not even the Eskimo dogs could find him here. Though the crevice was deep, there was a ledge wide enough for him and Tonda to travel side by side. It was growing more and more painful for him to walk, so he lay down and tried to lick his wound, but it was too high up for him to reach. His eyes burned as the rage within him mounted. The zinging bullets and the pain in his shoulder, now spreading throughout his body, brought back tragic memories, memories that made him want to rip and tear and kill.

Tonda backed away. This was a different Atu. She watched him intently as he gave voice to deep, rumbling growls and groans. In his pain and anger she wondered if he would hurt her.

Atu forced himself to go on, following the ledge to an even deeper crevice. By now his shoulder was stiff, and he walked with effort, limping painfully. As the pain mounted, his growls were more like groans forced out through gritting jaws. He shook his head and snapped his long teeth, as if he were biting at invisible insects. It was another way of expressing anger toward enemies he did not know how to fight, enemies with booming sticks that struck death.

Atu followed the crevice until he came to a wider ledge where he lay down. Closing his eyes, he groaned. Tonda sat beside him, uncertain what to do. Then, moving closer, she began to lick his torn shoulder. Gradually his rage quieted. Only the burning, throbbing pain was left. Tonda made a singing noise in her throat, as if trying to comfort him. He growled in return, a low growl that told her he understood.

For several days Atu's shoulder ached and throbbed and his body felt feverish. He was too ill to make any effort to move. Though the bullet had not broken any bones it had torn through the shoulder muscles, opening the old wound again. Tonda hunted along the icy ledge, digging out little shrimp-like creatures, frozen fish and mollusks. She even found sea weeds that tasted good. She offered the fish to Atu, but he would not eat. Her little black-tipped nose nudged him lightly, insistently, for it bothered her that he kept refusing food.

It was several days before Atu felt like eating. When his appetite did return he gulped down all the fish Tonda brought him. He was so starved that he failed to share them with her. But she understood, and was wise enough to eat her food before she brought him any. Day after day she licked his shoulder until it began to heal. When the pain lessened he got up and walked around slowly, carefully, trying out his shoulder muscles. As soon as the stiffness and swelling was gone, he was ready to leave the cavern.

Limping slightly, he went to the plateau again. He stood sniffing the cold air, trying to catch the odor of his human enemies. But he did not scent anything that made him uneasy. The air was filled only with signs he understood. Feeling safe, he led the way across the plateau, Tonda by his side.

April brought warmer weather, for Sukanuk was gradually rising higher in the sky. By the middle of June the island hills were covered with grass and flowers, the ice fields were beginning to break up and seals lay on the floes.

Atu led the way to his favorite island. Here he and Tonda fished in the tundra stream and wandered over the hills looking for birds' eggs. At first they were plentiful, but there were so many bears on the island that the eggs soon disappeared. Atu remembered the sweet-tasting roots and they dug for these, making the dirt fly. The bears spent long hours scratching their rough winter coats against boulders that were covered with willow vines, polishing them afterwards with their rough black tongues.

By fall, Atu and Tonda were sleek and fat. Once again the Arctic winter found them huddled over an Atluk, or wandering back and forth across the ice fields, searching for game. They were partners, sharing their catches, never quarreling over the size of a meal.

Atu was now three years old, and big for his age, weighing well over five hundred pounds. Tonda was two years old, and weighed almost three hundred pounds. Though still in the cub stage, she was growing more and more independent, and kept wandering away whenever she was in the mood. It was always Atu who looked for her. She never looked for him. Sometimes when he found her he slapped her lightly, just to let her know who was boss. But she never took offense. She bunted him in return, as if sorry she had annoyed him. Then, at the first opportunity, she would go away again. This happened over and over, throughout the winter and the following spring and summer, with Atu growing more and more mystified.

One day, he found her sitting on an ice pan watching him. For the first time since the beginning of their friendship she looked annoyed at his presence. Atu climbed up beside her and bunted her harder than usual. She slapped him right back. He raised his paw threateningly, undecided what to do. Tonda shot him a sullen glance, growled, then slid into the water and swam away. Atu followed even though he knew she did not want him around. Every time he got within touching distance she slapped at him and blew through her nose. Her actions were certainly mysterious. He understood them even less

when she found several females her own age and
went off with them.

Atu refused to be left behind and was deter-
mined to win Tonda away from her new friends.
But as the warm summer days passed he had to
accept their changed relationship. Tonda no longer
wanted him as a friend or protector. It seemed she
had other plans, and they did not include him. It
was only when she and her friends tried to fight him
that he suffered his final indignity. He was forced
to recognize the fact that he was no longer wanted.
He watched her walk away with the females, not
sensing that Nature had brought them to this part-
ing. From now on Tonda would wander alone,
or with other female companions, until she mated.

At first Atu missed Tonda's companionship,
but when winter came he almost forgot her he was
so busy trying to stay alive. He caught glimpses of
other bears, all of them intent on finding game.
Only the mother bears and their young stayed
together. The young males and the old males liked
to wander by themselves. Even the young females
were independent, going their separate ways. The
only bears that hibernated were those who were
going to give birth to their young.

Atu wandered through the dark winter days

and nights entirely alone. He searched for seals near the icebergs, digging under the small rounded hummocks, hoping to find a warm meal. And one day he found a mound of yellowish fur heaped on the ice.

Sniffing carefully, he circled the mass. Before him lay the rogue bear, Wonchonka. They had met again. Only this time his enemy seemed on the verge of starvation and quite helpless. He looked up at Atu with dim, almost sightless eyes, one forepaw raised in weak protest, as if he expected to be killed.

Atu retreated. Wonchonka was tricky. When he was at a safe distance Atu stopped and looked back. Wonchonka was still lying down, making no effort to follow, nor did he raise his head to see where Atu had gone.

Atu watched him for a long time, uncertain what to do. Though he neither liked nor trusted the old bear, for some reason he himself did not fully understand, he could not desert his enemy. Nature was more than hard on weaklings in the Far North. Only the strongest survived. He sensed the old rogue was dying from age and starvation. His own instincts of survival, so strong in his efforts to stay alive, overcame his fear and repulsion. It seemed he could not leave the old bear lying helpless on the ice.

Atu returned to Wonchonka and walked around him several times, watchful for a trap. But this time he knew that the old bear was not shamming. Atu growled. The growl was not one of anger. He was telling Wonchonka to get up. The old bear raised his head slightly, sniffing Atu. He acted as if he did not recognize his one-time opponent. Sensing that game must be brought to Wonchonka, Atu hurriedly dug around the iceberg, hoping to find a seal.

Thus began an unusual companionship.

Throughout the winter Atu shared game with Wonchonka, but he never learned to like or trust him. He knew the old bear could be dangerous.

When the February twilight hours of day

arrived, Atu sensed that his white world would soon
be teeming with life. It was the beginning of the
time of year that he liked. Gradually he made his
way north, toward Smith Sound at the head of
Baffin Bay. The journey was leisurely, for Wonchonka could not travel fast. He lay down quite
often, sleeping for hours at a time. Atu never lay

beside him, but chose a safe retreat on piled up chunks of ice, out of the reach of Wonchonka's claws.

The old bear seemed little interested in what went on around him, walking with head down, his steps stumbling and erratic. But when Sukanuk rose higher in the sky and grew hotter, he was more alert. Even his sight seemed less dim. Instead of following Atu, he often led the way.

Soon birds were returning to the Northland in great flocks. The sea, now breaking up into floes of all sizes, was dotted with thousands of Silqwa, or sea pigeons, and the sky was filled with little Arkpoodearq, the dovekies. Everywhere Ahpoo, the snow, was melting. Ookjuk, the bearded seals, too lazy to keep open their own Atluks during winter, were using the natural openings in the ice to reach the shallow water in the bays. Except during the mating season, they lived alone on the ice not too far from land.

Wonchonka took to the water. He did not swim fast. His great body looked as if it were floating. As the two bears followed the coastline, Atu dived for fish, eating all he could catch. But Wonchonka would not eat. He seemed to have only one purpose in mind, to examine each floe they came to, then he would go on. Eventually he found one to his liking

114

and climbed aboard. This effort seemed to take most of his strength and he lay stretched out, panting.

Atu watched him for several minutes before he approached the same floe. As he sank his claws into the ice and started to pull himself up, Wonchonka, eyes burning with hate, rolled over and lashed out with all of his remaining strength, his long black claws just missing Atu's head and throat. When the old bear saw that he had failed to kill Atu, his body shook with anger. Roars of defiance and defeat bellowed from his throat—defiance at a world he was so soon to leave, and defeat, because at the end of his long, battle-scarred life he had been unable to destroy the one bear he so intensely hated, the one he had never forgotten.

Atu swam around watching Wonchonka. The old bear was now sitting on his haunches, his body swaying slowly back and forth, growls of frustration still bellowing hoarsely from his throat. Gradually, his growls grew shallower until his body slumped forward and he lay in a motionless heap.

The scent in the air told the story. Atu knew his old enemy no longer needed him. Wonchonka was dead.

CHAPTER 10

Mating Time

Atu felt lonely. Although he had never liked or
trusted Wonchonka he missed his company. Now
that Atu was alone again he grew restless, scrappy,
always wanting to fight. It was not difficult to find
bears willing to oblige him. He did not mind being
clawed and torn. Scars were badges of honor. He
had never done any real fighting before, so his bat-
tles were tests of his strength. One thing he learned
about himself—he was strong.

Atu was now five years old but he was unaware of time as a measurement for growing up. He was also unaware that he was being discussed in the igloos of the Smith Sound Eskimos. Nannuksuak! Big bear! he was called, a real Ice King. Many times he had been sighted, many times hunted, but always he was gone before the dogs or hunters could corner him.

One Eskimo named Omah was sure he had shot him. "Last season I saw him with a smaller bear on the ice foot and shot at him. I know I wounded him for later there were streaks of frozen blood on the snow. My dogs trailed him for several miles, then lost him. He vanished, like a shadow," Omah said. He shrugged his shoulders, but his voice was tense and dramatic.

And so the stories continued, stories that dwelt on Atu's size, and the long, ragged scar on his shoulder, the scar that always identified him. How had he gotten it, they wondered.

"Perhaps my bullet ripped his hide!" Omah said hopefully, sure that his gun had been the instrument of success.

"Then he is not a shadow!" his friends teased him.

But the story that persisted, one gruesomely thrilling, was about Omah's cousin and Nannuk-

117

suak. Omah told this story over and over, his voice harsh with emotion. "You see," he would say, "my cousin had been hunting seals all day and when he rounded a turn in the ice foot this big bear leaped out at him from behind a snow mound and attacked him, mauling him so badly that he died later. The bear, strangely enough, did not try to fight the dogs, even though they growled and barked madly, so my poor cousin crawled back to the sledge and the dogs took him home. All this he whispered to me as he lay dying. 'Nan . . . Nan . . . ' he kept repeating. And I know he meant the *big* bear, the one with the scar on its shoulder, now turned man-killer!"

His listeners always shivered. Such a terrible way to die! But they knew it could happen. Ice bears had been known to stalk and kill human prey in winter.

Komi's father heard the tale and thought Omah's cousin had been a stupid fellow to have gone seal hunting alone. How could Omah be sure it was the bear with the long, ragged scar on its shoulder? Mumbled words of a dying man do not always make sense, especially when a man is barely conscious. Omah could have been mistaken. But once a bear gets the name of man-killer the news spreads rapidly, and Omah would be sure to help the story along. Since Nannuksuak had been seen in three different areas, a triangle that gave the Eskimos the pattern of his wanderings, they would not rest until the Ice King was found and killed.

"I do not believe that Ahtuckta is a man-killer," Komi said indignantly.

"It is hard to tell," his father replied. "Hunger, or being wounded, could turn him into a killer. We only know one thing about him. He is no longer a cub, but full grown, and an enemy of man. If he cornered us he would not hesitate to try and kill us. You must not call him Ahtuckta anymore. You still have dreams in your eyes about that bear."

Komi knew his father was right. He *did* have dreams in his eyes, memories that even now made his heart beat faster. His affection for the little bear was something he could not forget, nor did he want to. But the playmate of long ago was now an Ice King, with instincts of the wild, a natural killer. Drawing a long, sighing breath he said, "Perhaps you are right, Father. But I do not like to think so."

His father patted his shoulder approvingly. "You and I are no longer children. We are men and must take our place in the world. Ahtuckta is no longer a baby. He has taken his place in the world. Let us hope we never meet him."

Atu could not know of the stories. Though he still carried the bullet in his shoulder that Omah was so vocally proud of, he was not concerned with his human enemies now. He was feeling an excitement he had never known before. Padding along in the May sunshine, his huge body rolled with a lazy motion. But he did not feel lazy. He growled deep in his throat and tossed his head. Life had suddenly taken on a new meaning. He was no longer interested in being alone. He wanted companionship, but not the companionship of other males.

At first he did not understand this strange emotion. But as the early spring days passed he began to sense that he was experiencing the natural instincts of his first mating season. This strong urge to claim a female for his own led him to search for Tonda. At any time since they had parted he could have found her, but he had never felt the need. Now he did. He wanted her for his mate.

Because of Tonda he made his way toward the ice fields of Kane Basin where he knew she loved to roam. The wilderness spread out before him, miles of gleaming ice and snow. As he walked along, adding his own huge tracks to the different ones already in the snow, his nose constantly sniffed the air.

With unerring instinct he went to where a group of bears were gathered together. Atu circled the bears. The older males looked at him and growled warningly. He kept his distance, but continued to watch the young females with interest. But not one held any attraction for him. He was waiting for Tonda. He knew she would come here.

It was not long before a graceful young female bear came padding across the snow. It was Tonda. He had found his playmate again. All the fondness he had felt for her when she was a cub welled up in his heart. He wanted her for his mate, and he would fight for her, even though she might turn from him afterwards.

Tonda did not act as if she were glad to see Atu. She barely glanced in his direction, then she walked into the center of the group of bears and touched noses with a big male.

Atu was furious. Roaring out a challenge to his rival he stepped forward.

As the two bears paced back and forth, back and forth, they appraised each other, their black tongues lashing out, lips drawn back, exposing long yellowish teeth. Their dark eyes were flecked red with hatred as they moved in cautiously for the attack.

Suddenly they lunged and their massive forearms hugged each other. Breaking, they circled and charged again, deadly claws ripping flesh and drawing blood. Atu sensed his opponent was a strong and clever fighter. One false move on his part could prove fatal.

Circling again, their huge bodies moved quickly, lithely, muscles ready to spring into action. Then they charged, tearing at each other with their sharp claws. They swayed back and forth, their bodies quivering under the strain of battle. Breaking again, Atu backed away. At that instant his rival lunged, catching one hind foot and flipping him over. Then he pounced, sure of his victim. But Atu rolled to one side so quickly that the long teeth and ripping claws missed him. Jumping to his feet, he met the next charge head-on, his eyes burning like live coals. At first all he had wanted to do was to defeat his rival and chase him off. Now he sensed that this battle was to the death. His opponent did not intend to retreat, or to let him do so. He must fight, not only to win Tonda, but to stay alive.

Making a quick break, Atu moved slowly backwards. Not once did he glance at Tonda, afraid to take his eyes from the deadly enemy facing him.

Atu kept backing up. Though he seemed to be retreating, he was in reality waiting for that split-second when he sensed the other bear was off guard.

His opponent kept following, a cunning expression in his eyes, as if he, too, were waiting for exactly the same break.

Atu's deliberate retreat seemed to goad the other bear into following with quickened step. Each waited for a sign of weakness, a false move that would make the other one the final victor. Unaware that Tonda was directly behind him, Atu backed into her, losing his balance. Instantly the other bear was at his throat and they fell on Tonda. A free-for-all followed, with Tonda, Atu and the enemy all rolling together on the snow.

Tonda was the first to scramble to her feet. This left Atu struggling with his adversary, claws and teeth ripping as each tried to force the other on his back. The battle was even deadlier now because of its lack of sound. It was only when Atu finally sank his teeth into the heavy folds of skin and fur of the bear under him, searching for the jugular vein, that a roar of pain and defiance cut the icy stillness. Atu's growls were muffled as he sank his teeth even deeper into the soft throat.

The roars of the other bear gradually choked into low, gurgling whines. His rapidly glazing eyes stared up at Atu, as if making one last appeal for mercy. Atu stared back. The hot, fetid breath of his enemy, mouth dripping saliva, barely breathing, unable to move, filled him with an exultant sense of power. It needed only one more crunch from his long, sharp teeth to put an end to this battle. But the will to live, the law by which his instincts were governed, was stronger than his hate. His powerful

jaws slackened their hold. Slowly he raised his head and stepped back, allowing his rival to get up. But he was watchful.

Though badly wounded, the other bear was still a killer. Snarling, he growled low as he paced hesitantly back and forth. But he evidently decided against resuming the fight, for he turned suddenly and walked away.

Now Atu looked at Tonda. Their eyes sought each other shyly, then she came over and nosed him. He licked her face lovingly. Bunting each other, they walked away, side by side.

The affection that developed between Atu and Tonda was deep and all-absorbing. He watched over her as if she were still a cub, fondling her, even slapping her lightly when she went too far away from him. Though he adored her, he was male enough to assert his authority, and she seemed to think this was as it should be, but it did not change her behavior. At times she showed a strange aloofness, an independence of action that puzzled and annoyed him, for even during their mating season she still liked to wander away when he was asleep.

They never stayed long in one place. In the early part of June they left Kane Basin and walked leisurely along the coast, a pleasant feeling of adventure warming their blood. There were many interesting odors in the air, all to be investigated. Seals would be scattered on the bay ice, sunning themselves. It would not be difficult to find a warm meal.

As they padded along a heavy fog drifted across the sky, settling on their yellowish-white fur in millions of tiny crystal drops, which in turn broke and trickled wetly from their bodies.

The following day a sudden storm came up. Snowflakes blew in their faces, and the sky turned dark, muting the sparkle and color of their world. The storm lasted throughout the day, and by evening drifts of snow were piled against chunks of ice. Afterwards, the sky was clear again and Sukanuk, high in the sky, bathed the Northland with light and warmth. Atu and Tonda were not hungry, so they curled up near each other and went to sleep.

Hours later, Tonda woke up. She yawned, flipped her black tongue in and out and yawned again. Then she glanced at Atu. He seemed deep in slumber.

She got up quietly, almost stealthily, and padded away, the urge to be alone suddenly more powerful than her desire to be with him.

Once she stopped and looked back as if she had decided to wait for him. But the ever-demanding restlessness of her nature drove her on. She knew Atu would follow. He always had.

CHAPTER 11

Timah!

Komi, his father and uncle were on their way home from a walrus hunt. The season had been longer this year because winter had been slow to leave the Northland. But the last two days had brought a sudden change in the weather, the early June sun was hot, and water pools were forming on the ice, so they were watchful for signs of thawing.

As Komi lay breast down on the sledge he held in his hand the end of the Peetoo, or slipping rings, just in case the dogs scented or sighted a bear. Then the dogs could be released quickly. How excited he felt as his team raced over the ice! He knew that the dogs sensed his excitement for not

127

once had he needed to crack the thirty-foot whip in order to accelerate their speed.

Komi's father and uncle were excited and expectant, too. Quite often ice bears were seen along the coast. If they could take one home their hunting season would be complete.

The sledges sped on, bumping against the ice, skidding around sharp turns, almost bouncing in the air, as if the carriers themselves could hardly wait to add the white carcass of a fallen Ice King to their load.

Though it was the end of the hunting expedition, the thrill never diminished. Each trip was a series of new and often dangerous adventures; the men always looked forward to its successful completion. Summer would soon be here, days when the long hours of sunlight would allow them to hunt for the eggs of the dovekies on nearby islands. Later the eggs would be cached in snow and left to freeze for winter food. The skin of the dovekies would be used for clothing, so all-important to them. It was a good time of the year for laughter and companionship.

Tonda walked along swinging her head and sniffing the air. Sukanuk was shining again. Seals would be on the ice. Now she was hungry, and her

nose followed the scent waves with delicate persistence. As her feet padded the ice with light, graceful footfalls, she made her way around small pools of water, stopping to sip their icy freshness. All sorts of interesting odors were in the air, but her nose was seeking the oily pungence of seal.

When she finally caught its scent she changed her course, traveling inland. It was not long before she saw her quarry lying in the sun beside its Atluk. A few low snow mounds were between them. She must keep the seal from seeing or scenting her.

It seemed a long time before she was within striking distance, closing in step by step, almost inch by inch. She finally secured the seal for her own and began to eat it. The blubber was rich, providing a satisfying meal. Soon the white foxes were gathered around, waiting for tidbits. But Tonda was unwilling to share her scraps. The meal had been small. She stopped eating only long enough to sniff the air, as if wondering why Atu had not joined her. She was so engrossed in finishing the last tasty morsel of fat that she failed to pick up the scent of approaching danger. It was not until she heard the sudden barking of Eskimo dogs that she looked up, startled. The dogs came running over the ice, the sight of her driving them into a frenzy of barking.

Tonda was paralyzed with fear. At first she did not know what to do, and when she finally decided to run, it was too late. The dogs had surrounded her and were biting at her hind legs.

Again and again she struck at them. But they were quick, too experienced, jumping aside and nipping her hindquarters, making her bawl with anger.

Confused, and growing more and more enraged, she kept turning around, slapping viciously at her four-legged enemies. But she made little headway. They would not let her alone. She was so busy fighting that she did not see the Eskimos coming toward her until they had surrounded her. All she could do now was charge head-on, and push everything out of her way.

And Komi's father was in her way. He had no choice but to raise his gun and fire. Tonda went down, killed instantly.

The Eskimos waited until they were certain that the white bear was dead before they ventured near it. Komi's father was sorry that he had been forced to kill the young female, but there was nothing else he could do. Touching the still warm body lightly with the toe of his boot, he said. "She has a fine pelt."

The men took out their long skinning knives

and prepared to remove the pelt and cut up the meat.

"Do you suppose she has a mate?" Komi asked.

"She's old enough," his father replied. "We'll keep a sharp lookout for one. The ice bear can sense when its mate is dead and will seek out her hide and kill for it if necessary."

"How do they know this?" Komi asked.

"Perhaps by the odor in the air. Perhaps in other ways. I am not sure. I only know it is true."

As the three Eskimos began to skin the bear, the dogs stood by, tongues lolling, as if expecting a piece of the meat.

Komi laughed. "You did not work hard enough for this bear," he said. "Besides, it is a female, and I will not give you the spleen. It would make you too brave. You would be fighting each other more than you do already. I can't have you acting like a mother bear with cubs!"

The three Eskimos laughed uproariously, thinking this an excellent joke.

When Atu awoke, he yawned, stretched and sat up. Tonda was gone again.

Shaking himself, he got to his feet and started off across the ice fields, his nose constantly scenting the air. The sky had cleared and Sukanuk glowed

131

warmly. No doubt he would find Tonda by some Atluk waiting to pounce on a seal when it came to the top for air. Finding her was only a matter of testing the breeze and catching her odor.

As he padded along he turned aside to sniff at what appeared to be seal holes. Soon he would find his mate. He could almost feel the softness of her body against his own as she reached up and licked his face. When he found her she would caress him in the same old affectionate manner, as if seeking forgiveness for having gone off alone.

Now he walked faster, his nose exploring the air. Suddenly he stopped. His head went up and his body began to quiver. He took a few steps forward, bit at his chest, then stood quietly, almost rigidly, for several moments. Tonda was dead. It was as if he could see her soft body lying crumpled on the snow. He began to tap the ice with impatient motions. Filled with grief and mounting rage, his movements quickened until he whirled and struck at everything around him, his great forepaws pounding the ice as he gave vent to his emotions in the only way he understood.

Intent now on finding her body, he started off across the ice fields. He had no sense of fear for himself. He would find her and take her away with him, and kill anything that stood in his way! He clipped off mile after mile, his nose constantly scenting the air. Many times he changed directions, for he was following her body odor.

As he came closer and closer to the traveling dog teams, he cut across low hummocks and padded over rough ice until he reached the towering cliffs. Here he followed the ice foot, his slender head swaying from side to side, a deep rumbling in his throat. The stronger the scent grew, the more violent he felt. He was careful to keep the wind in his favor, not wanting the dogs or his human enemies to learn of his presence.

It was not long before Atu saw the Eskimos and their dog teams and followed them all the way to the igloo on the hillside. Still careful to keep the wind in his favor, he hid behind a snow mound. He watched the Eskimos as they unhitched their dogs, tied them to boulders and tossed them large chunks of walrus meat. The dogs gobbled down the meat almost instantly, whining for more.

As Atu checked the hillside and watched the dogs and men moving about, a strange feeling stirred within him. He wondered if he had been here before. But memory was dim. Its ghostly touch passed as quickly as it had come. He was here for one purpose only, to take Tonda's body with him, even if it cost him his own life.

133

Carefully observing the surrounding area, and the way to the sledge, he saw that he could not slip in unseen. He would have to go in openly. He did not hesitate. With great forward leaps he was up the hill and at the sledge before the Eskimos were aware of his presence. His long black claws ripped right and left, tearing at the leather thongs and cover. When he found the roll of fur underneath he pulled it out and shook it, as if he would force it to come to life. And he kept on shaking it until it opened up like a shaggy white flag. Then he buried his big head in the soft fur.

Komi and his father watched in amazement. They had heard many times of the ice bear's deep affection for its mate, an affection that now was a rare and sadly touching experience to witness.

It was Komi who suddenly nudged his father excitedly.

"Look," he whispered. "On the right shoulder. It is Ahtuckta!"

His father could see the long, ragged scar. He shook his head in amazement.

"No one is to kill him," Komi ordered, his voice hoarse with anxiety. "The young female was his mate."

"I won't shoot unless I have to," his father replied quietly. They needed the hide of a bear

like this; it would provide robes and pants which were a necessity at all times. But Komi's father shared his son's distress.

At that instant Atu looked at them. His small dark eyes were filled with grief for himself and contempt for what these human enemies could do to him. A long, long silence followed. His enemies did not make a sound. The dogs were strangely silent, too, as if they sensed how dangerous it would be to bark.

Atu's stare grew more and more insolent as he waited for guns to boom in his ears, guns that would put an end to his life as they had to Tonda's. But the guns did not boom. His enemies stood motionless, staring back at him until he sensed that they did not intend to kill him. With a deep, rumbling growl, he picked up Tonda's hide, pulled it to one side, and turned to leave.

It was then that Komi's uncle came out of the igloo. When he saw Atu he grabbed his gun and shouted, "It's the man-killer! Shoot him! Shoot him!"

"No! No!" Komi screamed, and stepped between Atu and his uncle.

Atu whirled, the sudden sharp sounds of their voices triggering his hate again. He stepped forward slowly, deliberately, ready to kill or be killed.

"Ahtuckta, Ahtuckta," called a voice, a voice that came like a whisper out of the dark canyon of memory. But it was enough to stop his charge. What was there about this voice that suddenly stirred him? He saw only a human enemy facing him. Yet there was something about the voice of this enemy that arrested his attention long enough to lull the terrible waves of hate racking his body. No longer certain that he wanted to charge, Atu began to tap the snow lightly with his forepaws. Tonda's pelt lay in a mound beside him. No one had tried to take it away. Confused, he wavered. The animal wildness in his eyes was veiled with indecision. Though instinct urged him to charge, some other emotion, deep and compelling, held him back, making him pause for one brief moment. Head raised, body tense, he stared intently at Komi.

"Ahtuckta, Ahtuckta," came the voice again, low, soft, strangely comforting.

Atu stood quietly, as if listening, then he turned slowly, hesitantly, picked up Tonda's pelt and started down the hillside.

The three Eskimos watched him until he disappeared beyond the snow mounds bordering the ice foot.

"You see," Komi said, looking at his father and

uncle, "he is *not* a man-killer! And he *did* remember me!"

His father smiled fleetingly, his stomach still shaking with nervousness. "I do not believe that he remembered you," he replied kindly. "He came to kill or be killed, but when we let him take his mate's hide he was uncertain what to do. It was stupid of us to take such a chance. He was so close you might have been mauled before we could stop him."

"It was stupid and soft," the uncle spoke up angrily. "Now we've lost both of them!"

Komi's father looked at his brother sternly. "We will say no more about it. It is Timah. Done. Finished."

Komi did not speak. Nothing his father might say would make him believe that the Ice King had not recognized him. "Good-by, Ahtuckta," he whispered. "Good-by, forever." It was Timah for him, too. Done. Finished. He hoped they would never meet the Ice King again. Next time, his father would not be so generous.

For several days Atu wandered across the ice fields dragging Tonda's frozen pelt beside him. He stomped on it with his forepaws, or caressed it with his big head, as if trying to make life and warmth return to the stiff, white fur. But no amount of

138

stomping or caressing changed the unyielding pelt. It was no longer his playful, teasing mate, but only a lifeless symbol of affection.

Sensing there was only one thing to do, he finally carried the hide out to sea where he left it to float, creamy-white, against the sapphire-blue of the water. Then he returned to the ice. For him, it was Timah. Done. Finished.

Catching the odor of seal he went hunting, hungry for the first time in several days. Once more he was a wanderer, searching, ever-searching for game. Soon his world would be hard and white and inhospitable again. He must get fat on his body for the long winter months ahead.

Glossary and Vocabulary of the
Smith Sound Eskimos of Northern Greenland

Ah-chook'!	*Right!*
Ah-ning-ah'-nah	*the moon*
Ah'-poo	*the snow*
Ah-tuck'-ta	*ice bear cub*
Ark-pood'-e-arq	*little auk or dovekie (birds)*
Atluk	*seal's breathing, or escape hole*
A'-wick	*walrus*
Eye! Eye!	*Stop! Stop! Used as a command when driving dogs*
How'-ah!	*Left!*
Huk!	*Ahead!*
Ice foot	*A collar of salt water ice formed upon the shore by the rising and falling of the tide.*
Ice pan	*A detached piece of salt water ice, one that has broken away from the fast ice.*
Igloo	*The real igloo of the Far North is made of stones and is partly underground.*

Kai'-git!	*Come here!*
Ka-lil'-e-wuk	*narwhal*
Lead	*A crack in the sea ice caused by the ocean swells running under the ice. It may be a few feet wide to several miles in width.*
Metik	*eider duck*
Nan'nuk	*ice or polar bear*
Nan'-nuk-suak'	*big ice or polar bear*
Nau'ya	*glaucous gull*
Net'sik	*little ringed seals of the Arctic*
Ook-juk	*bearded seal*
Ook'-pik	*white Arctic owl*
Oo-kud'-a	*white Arctic hare*
Pee'-too	*A rawhide rope which runs through the ivory rings on the ends of the dog traces, binding them to the sledges.*
Silq'-wa	*sea pigeons*
Suk'-a-nuk	*the sun*
Tah'-ta-ra	*Kittiwake gull*
Ti'mah	*Done, finished*
To-koo'!	*Look!*
Tok'-suk	*igloo entrance*
Too-a-vit'!	*Hurry up!*

ABOUT THE AUTHOR

Ernestine Byrd was born in California and has lived there ever since. Her interest in outdoor life and nature study led to a writing career that began when Mrs. Byrd was sixty years old. She has a son, a daughter and two grandchildren.

About ICE KING Mrs. Byrd writes: "A continued interest over the years in the polar or ice bear grew until I felt I must write a story about these unusual bears. Reliable research material was difficult to find, but I refused to give up. Learning about Northern Greenland and the Smith Sound Eskimos was equally stimulating—the entire research was rewarding to me and I hope to my readers."